Seasons Of The East Coast

Summer Kind Of Love

CHARLÈNE BOUTIN

Cover illustration by Sierra Ward
Editing by Swati Hegde
Copyediting & proofreading by Dark Grove Press
E-BOOK ISBN 978-1-7382847-0-2
PAPERBACK ISBN 978-1-7382847-1-9
www.irisbookspublishing.com

To my son, Marshall:
For giving me a newfound purpose and helping
me rediscover the love of writing again.

Author's Note

Summer Kind of Love is intended for 18+ readers. It contains explicit language and swearing that some may find offensive, as well as on-page sexual content.

While I wrote this book with the intention of warming your heart and making you smile, it does tackle some heavy subjects to get there, which means there are a few scenes and subjects that may be upsetting or triggering for some readers. If you are affected by any of the following topics, this may not be the best time for you to pick up this book. If you do, please proceed with care and caution:

Toxic/strained relationship with a parent

Themes of loneliness, depression, and burnout

On-page anxiety symptoms, meltdowns, and anxiety attacks

On-page suicidal ideation brought forth by extreme anxiety attacks

Brief depictions of alcohol consumption

Brief mentions of childhood bullying.

Chapter 1

The rain's soothing dribble against the window is the only thing keeping me calm as my finger hovers over the mouse. *Just click it*, I repeat to myself, over and over again, trying to ignore the frantic thumping of my heart against my ribcage. *You know you've got to do this.*

Blinking back at me on my laptop's screen is the final step of the booking process for Glendale Beach Resort's oceanfront single cottage. It shouldn't be such a big deal, but the slight trembling of my fingertips and single bead of sweat on my forehead tells another story.

"Goddammit, why does everything have to be so hard?" I sigh as I push the laptop away from my thighs. Ever since Dad left, it seems like I've been asking myself this question more and more often.

I quickly look around my living room/kitchen/dining room. From the window to my left, several office windows

light up the evening at the next-door Concordia University building, where people I assume to be professors are nervously typing and staring back at their own monitors.

If they were to glance at the run-down twelve-storey apartment building to their right, there's a chance they'd see me echo their own anxious existence.

I don't know why I bother, but I move my finger away from the keyboard and pick up my phone instead. Who knows—maybe Dad will pick up this time and give me the encouraging push I need.

The ringtone echoes against my ear, and my breath halts in anticipation. Maybe this time…

It's been an entire month since Dad stopped responding to my calls, which so happens to be the same amount of time since Jasper dumped me. In fact, Dad hasn't responded to anything I've sent him since that day. Worse still, he hasn't *seen* my DMs on social media, which means he hasn't even logged on in months.

The first time he didn't answer—when I called him in tears about Jasper dumping me—I didn't get too worried. I cried out my broken heart alone, and I was pissed, of course, but nothing more. Plus, I'd called Sophie, my best friend, right afterward, and she'd rushed to my place with her newborn baby and a pint of Ben & Jerry's ice cream in tow. After all, Dad works a lot, so he could have been in an important meeting or something.

At 9 p.m. Sure. That's what I told myself back then, at least.

But when he still didn't respond to any of my calls, texts,

or DMs throughout the following week, that's when my anxiety rightfully took over. I can't just pop by his place for a quick wellness check. Ever since he divorced Mom about two years ago, he's been living in Colombia—the same place he works. Mom never wanted us to move outside of Canada for his work, and he finally got to do it after cutting us loose.

The phone continues ringing. At least I know he's alive. Andrea, his new girlfriend, responded to my DMs when I frantically messaged her about Dad. But she doesn't know a word of English or French, and I don't speak any Spanish, so our Google Translate-powered communication has been a bit muddy.

My heart stops in my chest when I hit Dad's voicemail again. *Should have seen that coming*, a voice grumbles in my head. I don't bother leaving a message, deciding to hang up instead.

"Okay, Avery," I say to myself while falling back onto my couch. "Enough self-pity for tonight." I whoosh out a breath, grab the laptop again, and in a single move, I press *Confirm Booking*.

There. It's official. I'll be spending the next month on the ocean shores of Cape Breton.

Alone.

Obviously.

I try to ease into the couch, but my shoulders feel too tight. I can't seem to get comfortable. The truth is, I want more than anything to get out of this apartment where every inch of space reminds me of Jasper, but the idea of spending an entire month alone has my heart in a vice grip.

Well, alone or not, it's what I need. And it's booked now. Can't take it back.

A sudden knock at the door jars me from the reverie of my spectacular accomplishment. I put a hand to my racing heart, which has never liked being startled. Oh, right. I told Sophie she could come over whenever she was ready.

"It's open," I say, my voice shaking slightly.

Sophie barges in, carrying a bag I now know as the 'Comfort Tote' in her slender arms. If the past month is any indication, she'll have filled this thing to the brim with chocolates, nail polish and accessories, face masks, and anything else she thinks I'll need for an evening of support with her. A zealous look of overexcitement twinkles in her big blue eyes.

She enters my tiny apartment, shuts the door behind her, and opens her mouth as if she's about to exclaim something, then stops as her eyes lock onto mine.

"You okay, hun?" she asks in a worried hush.

I take a deep breath to steady the shakes that have overcome my entire body. "Oh, no big deal," I say nonchalantly. "Just spent $4,000 on a seaside cabin in Cape Breton."

Sophie's already wide eyes go even wider. "Excuse me?" She takes two gigantic strides towards me with her effortlessly long legs.

I stand up to meet her face-to-face and help with her bags. She towers over me. "Do you think it was a mistake?" I ask without meeting her gaze. I don't know why I even ask, considering she doesn't know my reasons for going in the first place.

Once Sophie's arms are free from the onslaught of shopping bags, she crashes onto my couch, frowning. "When did you book it for? What are you gonna do? Who are you going with?" She knows I don't intend to invite her. Not that I wouldn't want to, but Sophie's youngest daughter, Heather, is barely four months old. It's definitely not the time for her to escape to Nova Scotia for a month with me.

I cringe in anticipation and shift my eyes to my interlocked fingers. "Monday. And … I'm going alone."

Sophie tightens her lips. "Monday … as in, this Monday?"

"Yep."

"Dude." She grabs my face and forcefully turns it so I have to look straight at her. "For that price, I better hope the place you rented is on a boat or something. Since when do you splurge $4,000 for a week away?"

I knew Sophie wouldn't approve. My stomach roils. "I wouldn't pay that much for a week."

She squints at me, suddenly suspicious. "Avery, how long are you going there for?"

I take a deep breath, preparing for Sophie's fury. "A month?"

Her face goes still. We stare at each other for what seems like an eternity until she explodes into a fit of laughter.

"What?" I ask, my brows furrowing. "I thought you were going to kill me."

"Come on," she gets out once her laughing subsides. She then lunges into a hug. I close my misty eyes, taking in the closeness. It feels nice. I hadn't realized how much I missed just being close to another person.

"I'm surprised, but hell, I'm proud of you," she squeals in my ear.

A warm fuzzy feeling spreads over my entire body. It's okay. I'm going to be okay. In the nearly sixteen years I've known Sophie, she has never once steered me wrong. Not even that time she convinced me to shave the side of my head to 'make a statement.' If she's okay with my month-long escapade nine hours from here, then I can't be too far off from making the right move.

Yet, I can't help the twinge of uncertainty that remains in the pit of my stomach. How can she approve when I haven't even told her why I'm doing this? I know she doesn't quite get my job or the emotional—and physical—toll a copywriting project can take on me. So I'm not sure she'll truly understand why I see no other way out of this.

I pull back from her hug and lean on my knees. Might as well embrace it since the booking is non-refundable. "You sure you don't want to know more before you claim you're proud of me?"

She shrugs and stands, heading to my kitchen. She grabs two hard seltzers from the fridge and heads back my way, handing me one. "A vacation's a vacation, Ave," she says as she pops open her can. I do the same and take a big gulp for courage. The cool, carbonated drink calms me down.

"Yeah, that's the thing," I say between two sips. "It's not technically a vacation."

"Avery, no," she drones, disappointment flashing across her face.

I can't help but smile. I knew the other shoe was about

to drop. Sophie has been bugging me to take a true vacation for years now, and we both know she's right about how much it could help me unwind. Especially after the month of heartbreak I've endured.

"It's okay," I tell her, feeling a bit more confident about my choice. Hearing Sophie's disapproval is enough for me to reconsider my approach. A bit of the weight has lifted from the pit in my stomach. "I'll take weekends off. Fall asleep to the sound of the waves crashing against the coast. It won't be all work and no play."

She rolls her eyes so hard I fear they're going to fall out of her head. "So what's the point of spending $4,000 to get away if you're just gonna be working all the time?"

I open my mouth to answer, but the words stay stuck in my throat. How do I explain this to Sophie? Yes, we've known each other for ages. In fact, there's probably no one in the world except my dad—and, to a certain extent, my mom—who knows me better than she does.

Well ... there is—or was—one other person. But I can't let myself think about him right now.

The point is, even though Sophie knows me inside and out, there are certain things I know she won't understand. It's not that Sophie isn't creative—quite the opposite. Her booming party planning business is proof of what she's capable of. But planning parties and writing copy are very different from each other.

They don't pull at the depths of your soul in quite the same way.

"Who's the client?" she asks before taking a sip of her

drink.

"Oh, you'd love them," I start. Instinctively, I shift into my happy mask. *Be excited. Show her you like this project. Love it, even.* "Prakriti Mountain Wellness. It's this Ayurvedic retreat center down in the States, in the Blue Ridge Mountains. They do a Panchakarma-style cleanse. Super spiritual. They need their entire website rewritten."

She squeezes her lips together. "Ooh, you're right. I'd totally go if I hadn't already planned our trip with Matthew and the girls this year." Unlike my painfully single self, Sophie's a mom to two beautiful girls. But apart from her swollen breasts that barely stay put in her pink tank top, you can hardly tell she gave birth four months ago.

In reality, Sophie defies every mom stereotype I know. When she announced her first pregnancy to me nearly four years ago, I feared I would lose her. She'd be too busy pouring herself into this new version of herself to make room for her best friend. And what if, when we did see each other, the baby would be all she'd talk about?

But that turned out to be the furthest thing from the truth. Sophie is exactly the same person she's always been. I absolutely love her eldest, Gwen. And Heather's just a baby, but I think I'd die for her regardless.

I won't lie and say I'm not a bit envious of Sophie. Motherhood has always been something I've dreamed of, more so than anything else, but Jasper wasn't ready back when we were together.

Now, he'll never be. At least, not with me.

A bolt of pain stabs through my chest. I managed

not to think about Jasper for an entire ten minutes—an accomplishment, really. But now my streak is broken.

Sophie probably notices my change in demeanour because she scoots closer to me and rubs my arm. "Oh, honey, I know." The entire reason she's here tonight is to not leave me alone as I navigate this shitty breakup. She's been coming over or inviting me to her place as often as she humanly can. Like I said: supermom.

I burst into tears without meaning to. Sophie hugs me close. "Things were going so well, Soph," I cry into her shoulder. "They really were." At least from my point of view. Jasper leaving me really did come out of nowhere, although the pain of it was no surprise. You don't get over a five-year relationship that easily.

If he had at least given me warnings or signs or told me something was up … maybe I could have fixed things. But when I'd begged him to give me an explanation or to reconsider leaving, he'd been absolutely clear:

No, Avery. I'm done. I'm moving on. So should you.

It's been a month since those poison-like words came out of his mouth, and the retreat website project popped up just in time to distract me and give me a much-needed boost of revenue now that Jasper would no longer help me pay the bills.

But I'd been staring at a blank page for an entire week now.

I was pulling from nothing. A void.

At that point, I had two choices: either I could give up and refund the payment for the project, which would leave me pretty much strapped for cash, or I could pull myself together and do the damn project, no matter how broken my heart and mind felt. Which is why I need this change of environment.

"I'm here," Sophie whispered as she stroked my hair. "You know I won't ever leave you, right? Unlike that asshole."

"I know," I sob. "And now I just booked a month-long *workation*, and I'll basically be broke." I would have been broke anyway if I'd said no to the project. Unfortunately, that change of scenery I need isn't free. But I'd rather be broke next to the sea with a project to do than broke in my sad one-bedroom with nothing but time to contemplate my failed relationship.

Plus, this dingy apartment reminds me of Dad almost as much as it reminds me of Jasper. Dad's the one who rented the truck and helped me move out of the university dorms, along with Mom and Jasper. I can't help but remember him crashing against the couch, exhausted after we'd finally gotten everything inside. Or how he'd taken us to his favourite Asian-fusion eatery after we'd all showered and changed from our sweaty clothes.

That, and I'm reminded of him every time I look through my window at the workaholic strapped to his office chair across the street.

"Well, I didn't want to comment on how expensive this place is," Sophie responded. "You know you've got a place to crash if you ever need it, right?"

The first thing Sophie had said to me when I'd told her about the Jasper thing—other than some obscenities about the quality of his character—was that she had a spare guest room if I had to move out and needed some time to find an affordable place.

But the idea of living nestled in my best friend's family, even for just a short while, fills me with dread. I love spending as much time as I can with Gwen, but I can't imagine going to bed and waking up in the same house as those two little girls.

Seeing Sophie tuck Gwen into bed while Matt rocked baby Heather would only serve as a glum reminder of how utterly single and alone I truly am. Of how much I stand out like a sore thumb in their perfect little family unit.

Of how much I hunger to have the same within my grasp.

But there is no way I can say that to Sophie. Best friend or no, some things are just out of bounds. And telling a woman who's four months post-partum that you're envious of her baby is just one of them.

I'll just have to make sure I have a new project lined up after this one so I can make rent.

So I force a weak smile and respond with a simple: "Of course."

God, I hope I'm doing the right thing.

Chapter 2

A loud hiss pulls me from the edge of sleep. I sit up from the backseat of my car and peek out the window. There's no one else in the Walmart parking lot except an old camper van, which looks exactly like the one Dad bought during the summer when I was nine.

I ignore the tightness of my chest and look around some more until I hear the hiss again. It's coming from the other side of the lot. I nervously shift to the passenger-side window and finally see the source of the sound: two cats hashing it out.

I sigh in relief and sink back into the cheap fabric seat of my Kia Rio. It's far from comfortable, but it will have to do. I've parked here in Woodstock, New Brunswick, to rest for the night, even though I've already taken several naps and stops along the way. I couldn't make it two hours along the Saint Lawrence River before stopping; I'm not used to driving

long distances.

This nine-hour trip is taking its toll on me.

The smart thing to do would have been to book a hotel room somewhere at the midway point. Perhaps Fredericton or Moncton would have been a good place to stop. But I've already splurged $4,000 on a month-long stay in a seaside cabin, so I'm counting my pennies and hoping I don't regret my decision.

Which is why I'm lying here, trying to fall asleep to the soundtrack of hissing cats in a Walmart parking lot, hoping that whoever is sleeping in that old camper van isn't some sort of creep.

My lips twist into a bittersweet smile as I recall the first time my family and I took the van out for a camping and fishing trip that summer. We took my best friend Logan along with us like we'd done the summer before, and he was just as excited about the camper van as I was. I shut my eyes briefly at the thought of Logan, willing myself to think about something—someone—else, but the memory persists.

That was the year Dad taught him how to properly fish, and that was the year Logan ended up catching more walleyes than me. Not that I was ever upset about it. The more fish Logan wanted to catch, the more often he'd come fishing with us, which suited me just fine.

The last summer before Dad sold the camper was when I started to notice something was off with him. One fishing trip in early August, when it was just the two of us, we headed out on the lake just before sunrise. We'd ventured into a new area of the lake, and while Dad was usually careful, he didn't see the rising landmass as he drove us forward. Before we knew it, the entire foot of the motor was ripped away with a violent impact.

Dad always dealt with a crisis in a calm and stoic manner, but not this time. Oh, no. This time his eyes went wild, like he was looking for an escape while we were stranded in the middle of the lake, and his breathing quickened in a way that scared me. It took a whole minute for him to respond to my cries of asking him if he was okay, for him to even acknowledge me at all. And although he managed to row us back to the shore without a hitch, his usual goofy demeanour was gone for the rest of the day.

It was only later that I connected the dots and noticed that was the point after which Dad's work trips away from home lasted longer and longer. How, even when he was home, he wasn't quite with us.

At least I had Logan to comfort me through it all. When I was with him, I forgot all about how heartsick I felt about Dad. At least, I did until we moved away the summer after.

It was years later that I realized my dad had a panic attack that day on the boat. I've become too familiar with the way they flush your skin, conquer your breathing, and make your heart want to rip out of your chest. Dad calls our shared anxiety disorder the 'family curse,' although it's always in a joking way.

I can't help but wonder what he's going through now. If he's okay. God, he's probably not okay. Otherwise, he'd respond to my calls or read my DMs or something. My heart clenches at the thought. If only he'd let me in. Let me be there for him.

I wonder what Logan would think of this whole thing. It's in moments like these that I miss him the most, even though we haven't spoken in seventeen years. But that's on me.

I shake the distant, but overwhelmingly real, memory of Logan and Dad away so I can fall asleep. It takes me a while to do so—my car is tiny, and even though I'm just under five feet tall, I wake up sore all over with a kink in my neck. Maybe staying in my car would have been a good idea a decade ago, but now that my thirtieth birthday is coming up, I don't think my body can swing it anymore.

Maybe if I was more in shape. I don't know.

The second day goes by in a blur. I barely register the majestic scenery that whizzes past me as I drive along Bras d'Or Lake, followed by Cabot Trail. My mind is too busy trying to keep thoughts of my breakup at bay.

Had Jasper been the most amazing boyfriend I could ever ask for? Not necessarily. Of course, we weren't 'perfect', but who was? He had his shit together, we shared a deep-rooted passion for *Terraria* and *Stardew Valley*—my two favourite video games of all time—the sex was good enough, and we both wanted kids. All that seemed like enough for me. More than enough, in fact.

I keep thinking back to our final conversation and can't make sense of most of what he said to me. Sophie thinks he's just making up excuses because there's another woman. But I've been low-key stalking his socials, and I've seen no signs of another woman in his life.

The last photo he appeared in was his friend's Instagram

story where they were enjoying a game night at Randolph's Pub with all the guys.

I wish there'd been another woman. If that was the case, I could have easily brushed off the things he said as excuses and lies.

I just can't do this anymore, Avery.

I'm so deep in thought that I barely register my phone's GPS announcing that I've arrived. I swerve suddenly to the left and brake roughly as I pull into the parking lot of what my phone is telling me is Glendale Resort.

I whoosh out a breath. Finally, I'm here.

I park the car and get out to take a look around. Right now, I'm parked near the resort's main lodge, which is a single-story building shaped like a mix between a U and a V. There's a wooden terrace on the right side of the main entrance, but right now it's empty, its tables and chairs stacked to one end.

On the opposite side of the parking lot is what looks like a motel. I know the resort offers regular motel rooms in addition to the hotel, suites, and cabins, and maybe that would have been the budget-friendly thing to go for. But I don't want to risk noisy neighbours or weird smells.

The true 'budget-friendly' thing would have been to go to the retreat—if the client would have been willing to sponsor my trip. But they weren't. Oh, well, I can't really blame them since it's our first time working together. I'll have to earn their trust first.

I'm frozen in place. My fists clench by my sides so hard my joints hurt. Part of me wants to go back and cancel the entire thing. It's non-refundable, but I haven't checked in yet.

Maybe crying my eyes out will convince them—I'm close to tears anyway. I can just go home, grit my teeth, and do my work like a normal person. I'll need to go home eventually, anyway. And I'll have $4,000 extra dollars to cushion my landing.

But home is where Jasper was. Everything in that tiny apartment reminds me of him. Even my desk, on which he bent me over on several occasions during above-average sex. I can't hole up back there and pump out copy for an entire website. Especially when the website itself needs to feel inspiring and life-changing.

There's no way I can channel those feelings in that apartment.

What other option do I have? Even going back to see Mom wouldn't work—Jasper had been to Mom's place way too often. I'd recognize him in every corner of her house just like I would in my apartment.

There was one other place I could go. But thinking about it is like a jab at my chest.

If Dad wouldn't even answer my phone calls, I doubt he'd react well to me showing up at the doorstep of his Colombian villa unannounced.

No. This resort is the way forward. Plus, this plan is Sophie-approved.

I check to make sure my car is locked, then walk into the lodge. A cool breeze of AC hits me and forces a shiver out of me. At first glance, the interior is clean. A scent of freshly done laundry hangs in the air, and the decor is minimal and tasteful. If this gives me anything to go by for what to expect for my cabin, I'll be pleased.

There's no one at the check-in counter. I look around, hoping someone shows up without me having to ring a bell or anything like that. Bringing express attention to myself isn't my favourite thing, but as the seconds pass in quiet waiting, angst starts building up in my chest.

My bones are weary from the two-day drive. And I have a lot of work to do in the morning. I inhale deeply and exhale out a sigh to gather the courage to ring the small bell on the desk.

It doesn't take long for me to hear footsteps from the back room coming my way. I steel myself for the usual awkwardness of encountering a stranger. My body tenses up just as a man strides through the doorway. It takes a second for me to meet his gaze, but when I do, my heart stops. *Oh my God.*

I didn't prepare myself for this. This isn't what I had in mind at all.

And I can see the thought registering in his warm hazel eyes as well. Seventeen years apart aren't enough to dull the recognition I see in them.

Standing behind the counter is Logan.

Chapter 3

The shock hits me like a tidal wave, drenching my bones with anxiety. I'd braced myself for several scenarios like I always do when I go somewhere new. The receptionist could be super rude. Or the inside of the lodge could stink of garbage. Perhaps, in some of my worst mental scenarios, a fire would erupt just as I walked in, and I'd have to save the receptionist from the burning building while avoiding certain death myself.

I can't yet process whether the actual reality facing me is better or worse than these scenarios. All I know is that panic seeps through me as I scrutinize every detail and expression on Logan's face at lightning speed.

How could he possibly be here? What sort of quantum universal coincidence would have brought him to Nova Scotia, of all places—and specifically, at this exact resort at the same time as *me*?

It's too much at once. The glee and dread collide in my chest and erupt like a colossal volcano, and before I know it, I turn away from him to escape.

I can barely feel my feet pounding against the gravel as I run, run, run. I can't breathe, but I keep going. My vision blurs and I'm almost certain my heart is going to rip away from my chest. I don't know where I'm even headed.

Anywhere but here.

Before I know it, I'm standing behind the motel building, my back against the wall. There's nothing but forest in front of me. My knees buckle under the weight of the moment, and suddenly, my *I can't breathe* problem becomes the opposite as I begin to hyperventilate.

Logan. Logan. Logan.

My entire body burns. I'm breathing as fast as my brain is chanting his name. Black dots appear in the corners of my foggy vision. Nails rake against both my arms, and I realize they're my own only seconds later.

I sense movement from the corner of my eye. A mop of curly brown hair and a warm radiance from his body. It can't be anyone else. Logan kneels next to me. *Shit. Shit. Shit.*

His hands grab mine and pull my nails away from my arms. "Avery," he whispers faintly. Or at least, that's what it sounds like. The thunder in my body is so deafening I can hardly hear it.

Someone's counting. *Three, four, five … one, two, three …*

I don't know how long it takes me to realize the countdown is coming from Logan, who's trying to guide my breathing—my hands and arms trembling under his touch.

My breathing starts to slow. The black spots fade from my vision. Next to me, Logan continues to count in a velvety voice. "—four, five … one, two, three, four, five …"

My entire body still feels like it's full of lead, and my heart is hammering away against my chest, but at least I can breathe normally.

I have no idea how much time passes like this, with Logan's voice guiding my body back to a state of … not so much 'calm' as 'not about to die.' Slowly but surely, the panic and dread reduce to my regular levels of anxiety, although the aftermath continues to wreak havoc on my body.

Logan stops counting. He's motionless next to me, and I sense his gaze burning through me. I can't look at him. Not yet.

Guilt rises through me—*why is he helping me?*—but I can't let my fears win again. I take another deep breath and close my eyes. This doesn't make sense. Of all the panic-stricken people on Earth, I'm the last one who deserves Logan's help. Not after the way things ended. After the way *I* ended things.

But the last thing I want to do is attack him with questions after he's helped me calm down. I finally deign to look him in the eyes.

A pang hits my heart. He's so familiar, yet so different. He still wears his glasses, but their thick rim is a style that suits him much better than the skinny ones he used to wear. His downturned eyes have the same spark, but there are new lines in the corners, just like mine. Long stubble now covers his cheeks and jaw, although I noticed a small patch where it hasn't fully grown in. A worried smile occupies his lips as he catches me staring.

Yet what stands out to me most is the familiar tingle of electricity I feel where his hands meet my arms.

Even though the worst of the panic attack has passed, the aftershock doesn't hold back. My body is weak after everything it has gone through, and without me being able to control it, the tears start pouring—his fingers reach my cheek to brush them away.

Suddenly, it's as if no time has passed at all. I'm thirteen again, having a breakdown before Christmas exams, and Logan is wiping tears from my eyes, his touch soft like a butterfly's wings. I'm ten, holding his hand tight as we jump together into the lake. I'm eight, alone in the schoolyard in a new town with no friends, and he's smiling at me for the first time, asking me if I want to play with him.

Somehow, we're still intact.

We're still friends.

I close my eyes to absorb the moment. But Logan's hand doesn't stay on my cheek for very long. He snaps out of whatever reverie we've been caught up in and pulls away. Still, his other hand remains on my arm.

"I'm sorry you still have to deal with those attacks," he says, finally breaking the silence, and for the first time, I notice his voice is nothing like the high-pitched tone I once came to know as *Logan*.

I shouldn't be surprised. Obviously, his voice changed. At thirteen, he was a late bloomer, so I don't know why I expected him to sound the same seventeen years later.

I open my mouth to speak, but no words come out. This is

a regular occurrence for me post-panic attack. It's like there's a disconnect between my mouth and my brain—I can move my lips, and I can form the words in my brain, but the two won't reconcile.

Logan knows what this is. So he nods silently and flashes a gentle smile. That's when I notice his teeth. He must have gotten braces shortly after I moved because they're now perfectly straight.

The smile does something to my insides. I can't recall the last time I've felt a twinge like this. And suddenly I'm giggling, the last of my tears falling away on my chin.

Logan laughs. Despite the change in his voice, his laugh sounds exactly the same, just deeper. It's throaty in a way that feels so genuine and contagious. Hearing this makes me laugh even harder, and before I know it, I'm leaning against his chest, unable to contain my emotions again. But this time, I'm on the opposite end of the emotional spectrum.

His scent is both familiar and different. I recognize the smell of clean cotton and soap from when we hugged as kids, but there's something new here as well. Something musky, comforting. And slightly salty, like the sea.

The warm tingle between my thighs wakes me out of my laughing fit, and I pull away as quickly as I leaned in. My laughter stops short, although I force an awkward smile to stay on my face to match his genuine grin.

"Sorry," I say in a voice that's shakier than I expected, although I'm relieved I can already speak. "And thank you."

"No worries," he says, his smile toning down a bit. "I couldn't bring myself to hope it was really you when I saw your name pop up in our reservation system. You probably want to get settled in your room—I can give you some space."

"Oh, right!" I exclaim, remembering the reason I'm here. I've rented a cabin. And Logan works here. *Logan works here. Why does Logan work here?*

"No rush," he adds, seeing that I'm still not a hundred percent back to myself. "We can talk later. I definitely want to catch up, but for now …"

"Yeah. Yeah." I slowly ease myself into a standing position, using the wall behind me as leverage.

"I'll stay quiet for now." I can't believe he remembers everything. My panic attacks started during the last school year we spent together: seventh grade. I still remember the horrible numbness and shakiness I'd felt in my body when I'd told him we needed to move back to my home city of Montreal. All because of my dad's job. And I remember how my heart melted for him when, despite his pain, he never wavered.

He was the one who gave me the idea to plan a seventh-grade graduation party to replace the eighth-grade one I'd never get. And he was there while I figured things out with how the panic attacks worked and how to best deal with them. Seventeen years later, he still recalls I'd rather remain quiet after an episode.

Most people would try to fill the awkward silence. But it only becomes awkward when someone feels that way. I'd rather just take the time to recuperate. And hanging out in silence with Logan was never an issue. We'd spent so much time together that silence was second nature after a while.

And for us, it was comfortable.

But today feels different. As he silently guides me to my cabin, I can feel that ease erode. It's been too long, with too many questions left unanswered. The silence weighs on my shoulders like a ton of bricks.

"I'll give you your own set of keys later, but for now, I'll unlock your door with my master key," he says once we reach the cabin.

Right away, despite everything, it's love at first sight with this place. The small red building is triangle-shaped with a small deck at the front overlooking the cliffs and the sea. As Logan fiddles with his keys, I can already see inside from the large window at the front—the triangle shape creates a high ceiling for the single room, giving it an air of effortless luxury.

I've even got a barbecue on the front deck, along with some plastic lawn chairs and a wooden picnic table. *Fun.*

Logan finally manages to unlock the door. He holds it open and steps aside, motioning for me to come inside. "All yours," he says with a tight smile. Whatever ease we had back a few moments ago is now gone, and he knows it, too.

Despite that, I slide by him to enter my cabin. It's clean, simple, and minimalistic, but lovely. To my left is a small kitchenette, complete with a stovetop and coffeemaker. The fridge is on the other side of the cabin to the right, and while it's not full-size, it's plenty big enough to allow me to stock up for a month.

The open space from the triangle ceiling makes the cabin feel airy and spacious. At the center of the single room sits a king bed that's whispering my name. I see the door to what's probably the bathroom to the left of the bed.

If I wasn't so shaky from my recent panic attack, and nervous from an impromptu encounter with the man who used to be my favourite person in the entire world, I'd be damn pleased with all this.

"It's perfect," I manage to say as I turn to face Logan. He's still holding the door, perhaps not quite sure what to do with himself.

"So …" He scratches the back of his neck. "I'm gonna let you settle in. Take all the time you need. Then you can come get your car, and I'll give you your actual set of keys." His eyes dart away like he's nervous. "And if you're feeling up to it …"

Even though the sight of him fills me with wonder and dread all at once, I know what he wants to say—and I want the same thing he's proposing. "Yes, Logan. I'd love to catch up."

A smile appears on his face. His eyes light back up. This is the Logan I know.

No, *knew*. "Awesome. We can grab a drink and a bite at the lodge. They have a patio. But like I said, no rush. I know how drained you must feel."

Although he's right about how exhausted I am, I also can't help but feel warm and fuzzy inside. Even after all these years, he's still so kind and caring with me. As if we were never apart. If it wasn't for his awkward stance and his grown-up frame, I wouldn't be able to tell any time has passed at all.

I force a stilted smile. Even though I'm excited to catch up, I can barely muster the energy to show it. "Okay. Sounds good."

"Great." He pauses, then gives me a quick nod. "All right. Take care." Then, within a moment, the door closes, and he's gone.

And I'm left to myself, with nothing holding me back from collapsing on the bed.

Chapter 4

I t takes me a solid hour to decompress from the shock of seeing Logan here and the subsequent panic attack. If I've got one thing going for me right now, it's the fact that I'm in one of the best possible places to decompress.

The sun is setting behind my cabin, painting the sky shades of purple and orange. At the front of the cabin, unobstructed by anything, is the sea. Its waves are angry and crashing against the rocky shore, situated below a short cliff that ends a mere twenty metres from my door. Already, the fog is starting to cloud the air.

The sound of waves has always been soothing to me. Although I never lived near the sea, it reminds me of my time in Red Lake, the place I lived for six years where Logan and I met. I can't count the number of times I let the faraway sound of the quiet shore lull me to sleep.

During plenty of these occasions, Logan had been there,

his quiet, sleepy breaths adding to the lullaby of the waves. And now, knowing Logan is nearby, it's impossible not to get thrown back to those moments in time.

One of my favourites happened over the summer between fifth and sixth grade when we went camping at White Lake, another Ontario lake named after a colour for some godforsaken reason. My parents liked to invite Logan along since his mom usually had to work through the summer. And while it was always fun, there was one day that stood above the rest for its combined perfection: beautiful weather, hot dogs on the fire pit for lunch, hours spent diving for mussels and sitting still in the shallow water waiting for minnows to tickle our toes, freshly caught walleye for dinner, and s'mores on the bonfire to wrap up the day. All of it with Logan by my side.

That day wasn't all sunshine and rainbows, though. Later, when my parents probably thought we were asleep, they started arguing in hushed tones while in their own tents.

"I'm not gonna let you just miss another one of Avery's Christmas plays," Mom said. Dad argued that every year was the same spiel and that it wasn't a big deal.

But we weren't asleep. We were both reading the first *Percy Jackson* book with flashlights underneath our sleeping bags so my parents wouldn't see through the tent's flimsy material. My heart sank once I understood what Mom meant, that Dad would yet again be gone on a months-long work trip instead of attending the Christmas play at school. And worse still, he didn't seem to care.

I pretended not to hear the conversation. But Logan

heard it just as well as I did, and as much as I tried to hide it, he noticed my slouched shoulders and resigned demeanour, even in the darkness of our tent.

Instead of acting like nothing was wrong, he took my hand, quietly unzipping the tent's door so my parents wouldn't hear, and pulled me along to distract me with a midnight swim. The sound of his laughter and the gleam of his smile in the moonlight feels as vivid as if it had happened just yesterday.

The thought of him gnaws at my heart. And it's not just because of my conflicting feelings about the last conversation I had with him. Shouldn't he be in San Fransisco? Unless he's on vacation as well ...

No, that doesn't make sense. Why would he be manning the front desk if he was taking a vacation? No, he is obviously working here for some strange reason. Even when we were kids, it was clear to everyone that Logan was a genius with computers. And even if I'd never admit this out loud—not even to Sophie—I periodically stalked him on Instagram to see if his life seemed to be going okay, once every few years. Maybe more. But who's counting?

Not me.

I'd been so stoked for him when I'd looked him up after graduating college. It so happened that he'd graduated too— from the University of Toronto, a long way from home for him. And he'd announced his move to San Francisco soon after. Obviously, some awesome tech startup wanted him for his software engineering genius.

Last time I checked, nearly a year ago, he was still in San Francisco, being his nerdy self and creating big things out of just ones and zeroes.

But seeing him here, now, has me worried. Not that there's anything wrong with working in hospitality; I respect the hell out of service workers. But the Logan I once knew despised spending more time than necessary working with most people. And there's no way his big brain could be getting the fulfillment it needs at a job like this, where the hardest technical challenge is probably a slight bug in the booking system.

I realize I'm getting ahead of myself. I've barely exchanged a full sentence with Logan. There's no way to know what's actually going on with him. Maybe he got married to a woman whose family owns this place, and he helps out occasionally while working remotely.

The idea of Logan being married sends my stomach reeling. Not that I have any claim to him. Not after the way I ran away.

I try to shake off the feeling but can't get my brain to shut up. Before I spiral into another panic attack, I decide to find a distraction.

And who better to distract me right now than Sophie?

I make my way outside and sit on the comfy chair placed on my porch. Before I call her without warning, I send her a text, in case Heather is sleeping. I've heard her rant about people who call or visit without warning several times now.

Her response comes barely a minute later:

Yeah call me now what's up?!?

Relief floods through me, and I immediately dial her number. When she picks up, I already feel a bit better—the power of friendship. "You won't believe who's working here," I say, slightly short of breath.

"Don't tell me it's fucking Jasper," she spits out, already angry on my behalf.

"God, no. I can't even imagine." That would just be perfect, wouldn't it? "It's Logan."

The other end of the line is silent for a few moments. "Logan, from Red Lake, Ontario? That Logan?"

"Yeah, that Logan." I can hardly believe it myself.

"What is he doing there? Didn't you say he lived in San Francisco now? Working as a programmer?" Sophie's voice turns high-pitched.

"Yeah, he—"

"Why the hell would he be working at a resort in Nova Scotia? It's literally on the other end of the continent."

When I can finally get a word in, I say, "I have no idea. You know pretty much everything I know by now."

We're both silent for a moment as I let her process the news. Although I haven't told Sophie about the social media stalking, she does know he was my best friend once upon a time.

"So … did he get hot?"

Of course that would be her first question. Heat rushes to my cheeks because I have indeed noticed how he's changed. How his jaw has squared out and he wears a nicely groomed stubble that suits him perfectly. How he has the same downturned eyes that glow with newfound maturity. How he's definitely a handsome man now, not a cute boy.

But that's not what I respond to Sophie. "Um, I don't

know," I stammer.

"That means yes." I can hear the teasing in her voice. "So, is he single?"

"What? I haven't ... I already told you that you have all the information I have."

"I hope he's single."

"He was my best friend."

"What has that got to do with anything?"

I sigh. I want to ignore what her words are making me feel. The slight twinge in my belly. The memory of his fingers grazing my face. And that night, years ago—

"Soph, I can't be with anyone right now," I insist. "I can't even contemplate being with anyone right now. I thought you'd know that better than anyone else."

"And I think you've paid your dues and done enough sulking. It's not like Jasper was good enough for you, anyway, or like you ever listened to me about that." I hear Heather squeal behind her, and I feel my heart clench.

"I remember," I whisper. Not that I ever agreed with her about that. "But I really thought it could have been my turn with him to ... to have what you have." My voice almost breaks at that last part, but I hold it together.

"Well, it's a good thing you didn't because he could have just decided to up and leave like he did for you here. And you'd be left as a single mom."

At least I'd have a baby. But I don't dare tell Sophie that. The last thing I want to do is guilt-trip her for having what I don't. That's not her fault; it's mine. Maybe if I'd caught on earlier that Jasper was going to leave—or if I'd been the person he needed—things would be different now. Maybe I should have listened to Sophie all those times when she was warning me about him.

"Anyway, I'm supposed to meet Logan for a drink later, and I'm so fucking nervous."

"Yeah, I can imagine. Just pretend it's me or something, only ridiculously more attractive to you."

I roll my eyes. "Har har."

The happy baby squeals have devolved into cries now. "I'm sorry, I think I'm gonna have to let you go," she says in a hurry. "But text me after the drinks. Keep me updated."

"Yeah, yeah, of course. Speak later."

I hang up, not sure whether my mood is better or worse than before. Before I go back to feeling like shit, I decide to get ready to walk back to the lodge. I've still got to get my car parked next to the cabin. Plus, Logan is expecting me for that drink.

Trepidation fills my body down to my fingertips. Even though guilt is still gnawing at me, I'm elated at the idea of catching up with Logan. Sophie may be my best friend, but I've never felt the same way around someone as I felt when Logan was in my life.

Seen. Understood. For who I really was. Really *am*.

I go back inside and step into the small but clean bathroom next to the king-sized bed. I give myself a quick glance in the mirror, in front of which I have to tip-toe to fully see myself. Horror strikes me at once. I'm an utter and complete mess— my long strawberry blonde hair is frizzy and knotted, likely from the beginning of my panic attack when I tend to pull on it. Deep bags underline my tear-swollen eyes, which reflect back a tired—rather than luminous—blue.

And this was Logan's first impression of me? At least I didn't wear mascara today. Otherwise, the tears would have smudged everything and made me look 150 percent more chaotic.

My first instinct is to look for a hair elastic in my bathroom bag, but it's still in my car. Instead, I try to finger-comb the tangled waves and flatten the frizz away. A cool splash of water calms the redness in my face, but it does little to erase the damage.

Oh, well. There's not much I can do about it except worry he'll think I've completely given up on looking good.

Which, I kinda have. I've just been dumped. But, of course, I'm not gonna lead with that. *Pathetic.*

I give myself a last once-over and head for the door as my heart keeps hammering against my chest like it wants to shoot to the moon. But as I touch the door handle, I pause.

I have no idea why I bother doing this, but I still do. It's worth a try.

I let go of the door and sit on one of the overstuffed chairs near the breakfast nook, grabbing my phone from my pocket. I open my texts and find the person I'm looking for.

Dad.

With a tiny spark of hope, I type away, sending each message without waiting for a response:

Dad, you're not gonna believe who I just came across.

It's Logan. You remember Logan? Of course you do. Just imagine my reaction when I saw him lol

Anyway, I'm feeling a bit nervous. I'm gonna go meet up with him now for a drink and I keep worrying about the last time I talked to him

I remember you were at home when this happened because you took me out fishing without mom to distract me after it happened

Remember how you caught that pike that was so big it wouldn't fit in the net LOL

I look at the string of text messages and wait.

Maybe today will be the day he sees them.

Maybe today will be the day he actually texts me back.

But, of course, he doesn't see them. For the hundredth time, I wonder if he even goes on his phone anymore or if he's purposefully ghosting me.

Like I always do, I switch over to text Andrea instead, Dad's Colombian girlfriend. Even though things get lost in translation, I'm still grateful to know that my dad is alive, at the very least.

But she won't tell me much more than the fact that Dad is supposedly fine, which I hardly believe. You can't be 'fine' and stop messaging your daughter out of the blue.

Hi Andrea! Let my dad know I ran into Logan today. He'll remember who that is.

That's all I send. But I don't even know if she's patching my messages through.

I wait for a moment, then feel my phone vibrate and read what she sent back. A quick Google Translate gives me this response:

Oh that's wonderful, is that a friend? I'll let your father know. I hope you're okay, honey :)

No. I'm very much not okay. Just like every other time I try to contact Dad, my stomach gnaws like it's been filled with lead.

This has been a long, long day. And it's not even over yet.

By now, nothing else is keeping me back, so I head out of the cabin. I let the door close and auto-lock, knowing Logan will give me a key soon anyway.

Outside, the mist has crowded the air and the sea ahead, and the sun has almost set. I make my way back to the lodge, which is a short three-minute walk from my cabin. The salty scent of the ocean breeze soothes my nerves. I close my eyes and inhale it with intention. I can feel my heart slowly calming down.

By the time the lodge appears in front of me, Logan is already standing on the patio with a drink in his hand, and my stomach does a somersault.

He waves at me, smiling from ear to ear. I smile and wave back, feeling a bit more confident than before. Unless he's faking his enthusiasm, he does seem really happy to see me despite everything. Perhaps he's not holding a grudge. Or, if he is, he's not letting it surface at the moment.

If that's the case, that'll be something *future me* can deal with.

"Hope you're feeling better," he says as I join him at the round table he's at. Currently, we're not alone at this patio; we're surrounded by three other tables of people, to whom I don't really pay much attention. Because all I can focus on is Logan.

Sophie was right. I can't help but notice how handsome

he's become. Unlike the last time I saw him in the flesh, he's now taller than me. Of course, that's no big feat. Although I'm close to hitting five feet, I don't quite hit the mark— something my dad always good-naturedly teased me about.

Logan himself doesn't seem super tall. It's difficult to tell since he's sitting down. But I'm guessing he must be five or six inches taller than me. He's still narrow-framed and lean, but I can see his muscles have filled out considerably. Even though he's always been an indoor person, it's obvious he's been doing at least some physical activity. Unless the muscles in his forearms just naturally pop out like that?

Warmth pools in my belly at this observation. *Geez, Avery, calm down.* But a magnetic pull, undeniable and strong, captures my attention the moment my eyes meet his. Even though his face is so similar, the new angles and his short beard are doing things to me that I can't explain.

I realize I've been staring for way too long without answering. He's giving me a quizzical look. "Oh yeah, sorry," I stammer, fidgeting in the cheap plastic seat. It's a bit too small for my liking—I'm not lacking in curves. "I'm still a bit out of it. But I'm calm." I gaze away from him and fiddle with my hands.

"Do you drink?" he asks as he stands. "I'll go get us something, but I don't know what I should get you."

"Hell, yeah, I drink," I respond with enthusiasm. But then I remember I just had a panic attack. I need to take it easy. "Got something fruity and not too strong?"

He raises one eyebrow. "Why does that not surprise me?" Since we were so young when I moved away, we never drank together. All we got when we were thirteen was a single, tiny cup of wine here and there at family dinners. And that one rum and coke at our graduation party—but I don't want to think about that right now.

That being said, my tastes in alcohol are similar to my tastes in other things, and sweet, fruity things have always been a weakness of mine.

I'm surprised he still remembers.

"I know just what to get you then," he says as he turns around. Before I know it, he's gone back inside, presumably to the bar and kitchen.

I take the moment he's gone as an opportunity to check in with myself. The last thing I want is to start panicking again just as we're catching up. But a quick scan of my body reassures me. Although I'm feeling tense from this social encounter, I don't detect any rising peaks in my emotional state.

Deep breath in. Deep breath out.

I tell myself to just focus on the moment and have fun. Even though there's a chance things could be awkward, I try to detach myself from the outcome.

Easier said than done.

Logan comes back with two drinks in hand: one that looks like a hazy beer, and the other like the summery drink of my dreams. It's got shades of orange and red and what looks like ice blended through it. The glass is reminiscent of tropical drinks. He even took the extra effort to add a little paper umbrella to it.

The glee must show on my face because Logan starts laughing right as he sets the drink in front of me. "I'll assume

I chose wisely, then?"

"You read my mind." I'm about to take a sip from the bright yellow straw when I stop in my tracks. "Wait, how much alcohol is in this thing?"

Logan sits and puts his own beer down on the table. "Usually the answer would be a lot. But I toned it down for you. There's just an ounce in there now."

Feeling pleased with that answer, I take a sip and perk up. It hits every note I look for in a summer drink—sweet, juicy, sour, bubbly, cold … and I even detect a hint of salty?

It's perfect.

I moan in satisfaction. "What even is this?"

Logan chuckles, obviously satisfied with my reaction. "It's the resort's specialty drink. The Cape Dream."

"What's in here? You've gotta teach me the recipe."

He smirks at me. "Um, absolutely not. It's a trade secret." He grabs his pint of beer and looks straight into my eyes. "We'll see how I feel at the end of your stay."

The end of my stay … I don't even want to think about that right now. Somehow, for an instant, I forgot this wasn't permanent. I don't live here. This is only a façade. A distraction from my mess of a life to allow me to get inspired to do my work again.

I'm not sure I like how this makes me feel. But I play along and smile, returning his gaze. "Oh, yeah? What am I gonna have to do to pull it out of you?"

A sudden image flashes through my mind: my hands all over Logan's chest, rigorously unbuttoning his checkered shirt to uncover the muscle underneath. Blood rushes through my cheeks.

Why did my mind go there?

Logan must notice my discomfort because he raises his glass to change the subject. "To old friends," he says simply.

I clink my glass with his, careful not to spill a single drop of this godly elixir. "To old friends," I repeat before taking another huge sip. My eyes roll almost uncontrollably from the explosion of flavour. Logan smiles, satisfied at my reaction.

"So," he starts after swallowing his swig of beer. He leans comfortably against the table. "What has Avery Breton been up to for the past seventeen years?"

"Well, that's a loaded question." I have no idea where to start. "You know … the usual."

He chuckles. "The usual? And what would that be?"

"Well, for starters," I begin with a deep breath, "I'm my own boss now. Well, kind of." I pause, expecting him to jump into the conversation, but he doesn't. Instead, he's staring intently at me. Listening. Like, *actually* listening. Waiting for me to continue.

This throws me off for a moment. I'm used to people speaking over me—even Sophie will interrupt me all the time, although she doesn't do it out of malice. She just can't contain herself.

"I write stuff for businesses, like, on a freelance basis," I explain. Telling people you're a copywriter typically doesn't pan out well. They'll either assume you're in copyright law, or they'll have no idea what you're talking about.

"Oh? What kind of stuff?"

"The words on their websites, social media, emails … that

kinda stuff."

"Oh, so you're a copywriter."

I'm stunned. "Yes, exactly!" I say with way too much enthusiasm. And now that he's started my engine, I find it hard to stop. "But this recent project is a doozie, so I needed a new perspective. Which is why I drove from Montreal all the way here."

"Ah," he says, giving an approving nod. "So why here in particular?"

"I always wanted to visit the cape I share a name with," I explain. I don't waste any time launching into my follow-up. "But I could ask you the same. I thought you were working in San Francisco."

Surprise hits his face. *Oops.* Now he'll know I've been low-key stalking him online. Or, at least, that I used to at some point.

"Well, um," he stammers. "I was. For a long while, actually." I can see him squirming in his seat a bit. Did I hit a nerve already? But he shrugs it off and continues. "Still am, actually. I just took the summer off to switch things up a bit."

"Okay, so why here?"

"That's easy." He motions with his arms as if showing me the entire place. "My uncle bought this place two summers ago."

"Ooh." So this is a family business?

He leans back into his chair to exaggerate his smug look. "Yup. I mean, he's never here, and it's all run by his manager, but still. It got me an in."

"Cool." There's a sudden quiet tension that fills the

evening air. Unable to let this silence hang for more than a few seconds, I spit out what's likely the most chaotic sentence I could utter:

"Actually, I lied—I'm not just here for a new perspective. I've got writer's block because I just got dumped last month and I needed to get away ..."

Oh my God, why can't I shut up?

"And if I don't do this project, I'll run out of money and lose my apartment." As soon as those words leave my mouth, air escapes my lungs. What is wrong with me?

A small bit of shock registers on his face. "Oh," he says, looking genuinely sorry. Now I'm mad at myself. The last thing I want is for him to pity me.

But he's not done speaking. "Was the guy an idiot? He must have been an idiot."

"Why?"

"He lost you," Logan says simply.

Heat flares down my chest. I look away, suddenly very interested in the material this deck is made of. There's something hanging in the air, and I don't know what's going on, exactly.

But it's obvious Logan and I are still connected in some way.

Chapter 5

The sun has fully set, and I find myself with aching cheeks from smiling way too much. We're still sipping our drinks, surrounded by the soft glow of lanterns that illuminate the patio. Most of the other folks are gone; only Logan and I, plus two middle-aged women, remain. The sound of waves crashing against the shore creates a soothing symphony, while the scent of salt in the air fills my lungs with each breath.

God, I love it here already.

And I just can't get over how easy it is to be with Logan. It feels like I never left.

Well, sort of.

He's very obviously a man now. I skipped out on his awkward teens and that early twenties phase when men are still growing into themselves. And I'm kind of disappointed I did because I'm reminded of exactly how much he mattered

to me. We weren't best friends by accident.

It was a good thing we found each other when I arrived in Red Lake with no friends and no knowledge of the English language. Logan didn't care if I couldn't speak English yet, or if I had weird tendencies like singing to myself in the playground or staring at the clouds in silence for long stretches of time. He was immediately drawn to me, and I to him.

Learning English was much faster when I could practice with a friend, and I was always there to scream at the bigger kids who constantly picked on him. And even though he'd tell me to stop sticking up for him, there was no way I'd leave him defenseless. Just like there was no way he'd leave me to fend for myself if our roles had ever been reversed.

I still remember the devastation in his eyes when I'd told him about our move back to Montreal. Bringing up this image twists my insides like a vice. Jasper dumping me felt horrible—it was one of the most painful experiences I've ever gone through—but it still doesn't compare to being ripped away from Logan back then.

If only we'd have stayed in touch. Instead, I went ahead and ruined it.

As the warm evening air turns cool, the familiarity of our conversation wraps around me like a heated blanket despite the bitter taste these memories bring back. I can't help but be proud of this man who used to be everything to me. He's living his dream career, and apparently, his performance has been impressive enough that they've granted him this summer sabbatical.

Not that it surprises me. He was always whip-smart.

"Your hair's gotten longer," Logan observes, reaching out and gently running his fingers through the ends, which are now long enough to touch my hips. His touch sends a shiver down my spine, and I can't help but hold my breath.

"Yeah, I've been letting it grow," I reply, suddenly aware of the electricity in the air between us. I want to ignore it because the last thing Logan probably needs right now is to become a rebound to a stressed out, just-about-to-turn-thirty mess of a woman.

"Looks good on you," he says with a smile, his gaze lingering on me for just a moment too long. I swallow hard, trying to brush off the flushed look on my face.

"Meh, it kind of washes me out," I deflect, bringing my eyes down. "I'm thinking of cutting it back to how it used to be."

He laughs, which isn't the reaction I'd been expecting.

"What?" I ask.

"It's just ..." He chuckles again. "Some things don't change."

"What do you mean?"

"I mean, you could never take a compliment, even today, when you're arguably the most beautiful you've ever been."

Forget being flushed. Now, the entirety of my body's blood supply rushes to my face. I must look like a red tomato. My lips squeeze together as my heart rate picks up. I push through, trying to find a way to shift the focus from me to him. "Well, you're not looking too bad yourself." I steal one glance at him and realize how much I mean it.

Logan is definitely not what some women would call a

'hunk.' And that's a good thing because that body shape has never been my type. I like my men strong but slender, with dark features and glasses, and that's exactly what I'm looking at right now. There's something endearing about his scruffy style and thick, curly locks. He's not tall, but he's filled out enough to have me imagining what it would feel like to bury my face into his neck and drown in his arms.

Yup. This grown-up version of my childhood best friend is definitely my type.

Oh, I'm in trouble.

"If you say so," he responds shyly.

"Well, well, well, now who can't take a compliment?"

"I guess neither of us have really ever been champions at that, huh?" He sighs and finishes his beer in one final swig.

I imitate him and finish off my own drink, then groan as I sink against the table. "Ugh. I need to get to bed so I can get up tomorrow and start this stupid website copy project."

"Wow, looks like you love your job," he remarks sarcastically.

"No, I do." I sit up straight again, wary not to look like the lazy, burnt-out writer I tend to feel like. "It's just …"

You're a fraud. You're not even worth a tenth of what they paid you. No one loves you.

"I need to write super emotional, transformational descriptions of this retreat so people can't help but book their stay right after reading the website," I say instead. "But it's kind of hard to write that way when all I feel is …"

Discarded like an old garbage bag. Like time is zooming by way too fast, and I'm shriveling up, and no man will ever want me.

"Hmm," Logan says, squinting his eyes in thought. "Less than inspired?"

That's certainly one way to put it. "Yeah, something like that." I gaze back towards the sea, which has calmed down by now. The moonlight dances across the calm surface.

Part of me wants to tell him how I really feel. But I have no right, not after how I treated him. I don't deserve to trauma dump all over him hours after we reconnected.

"I've got an idea then," he says with a grin, his hand resting on my arm.

"Oh?" I can't decide whether to focus on his burning gaze or his warm touch on my arm. He's looking at me as if he cannot see anything else.

It's dizzying.

And confusing. He's acting as if nothing ever happened between us that night.

"How about you let me take you on a tour of some inspiring activities around the coast?" he suggests, his eyes sparkling with enthusiasm. "I mean, you can spend the month in your cabin like a hermit and just stare at the ocean. Not a bad choice, in all honesty. But since we're both here, and since I've been here for a while now, I don't see why you wouldn't take advantage of it."

His genuine desire to support my creative process warms my heart. But beneath the surface, I'm flooded with doubt.

It's not that I don't want to spend time with him. Right now, I'm resisting the urge to meet his thoughtful gesture with a close embrace. I'd want nothing more than to feel his arms around me again, especially now that his forearms are tantalizing me.

But things can't be like they were before. I already know that just by how taut the air feels when I'm near him. And the last thing I want is for me to succumb to those feelings and use him like a rebound.

Use him like I did that night.

Plus, I am not ready for the inevitable moment he dumps my ass when he realizes how much of a mess I still am.

With a shaky breath, I force a smile and shake my head. "Logan, that sounds lovely, but I don't want to be a burden or take up too much of your time."

"Are you kidding?" he replies, his eyes widening in surprise. "Avery … I'd love to do this with you. How am I not going to jump at the chance to get to know my best friend again?"

But the more he insists, the stronger my resolve becomes. My hands clench into fists, hidden beneath the table, as I fight the urge to give in to his offer.

"Really, Logan," I say softly, avoiding his gaze. "I appreciate the thought, but I'll figure things out on my own. I don't want to impose."

He studies me for a moment, his eyes searching mine as if trying to uncover the truth behind my words. "I already told you that's not an issue. So what's really going on?"

I take in all of him—the curve of his smile, the way his hair catches the moonlight. It's difficult to describe how it feels to be around him—*me*, someone who's a sucker for words, can't find the words to pin him down.

But the closest I can find is *home*.

A cool breeze brushes against my skin, carrying the scent of salt and sea. I shiver involuntarily, but Logan's hand on my arm warms me instantly. "You can tell me to fuck off if you want to." There's a teasing smile on his lips.

My heart skips a beat, and I'm suddenly very aware of his fingers gently gripping my arm, sending sparks racing through my veins.

Even after the way I abruptly shut things down between us, does he really still want to spend time with me?

Maybe he does. Maybe, after all this time, he's forgiven me, even though I never asked for it. That would be such a Logan thing to do.

Swallowing hard, I manage a weak smile. "I'm not going to tell you to fuck off."

"Okay, good, because I was bluffing. I would very much hate for you to tell me to fuck off," he replies, releasing my arm but not breaking eye contact. We sit in silence for a moment, feeling the heat between us, before he grins and leans back in his chair.

"Okay," I agree quietly, my voice barely above a whisper. "Let's do it."

"Deal," he declares, extending his hand for a handshake. I take it, feeling the electric charge between us once more, and we seal our promise with a firm grip.

Our gazes meet, and I almost drown in the depths of his hazel eyes. The desire within me is so strong that I could cut through it with a knife. And instead of shying away from it, I allow myself to fully experience it. Even if I have no intention of acting on it, just letting this want for him wash over me feels nice.

At least, it's nicer than anything I've been feeling over the last month. For the first time, I'm starting to feel like it's possible to long to be in the arms of someone other than Jasper.

Even if it's just to fantasize about.

Chapter 6

The morning sun filters in through the gauzy curtains, bathing the cabin in a soft, warm glow. I blink awake slowly, stretching my arms over my head as the faint cries of seagulls drift in through the open window. The crisp ocean air kisses my skin, invigorating me for the day ahead.

For a brief moment, I'm completely calm.

Then I remember why I'm here, and the anxiety creeps back into my chest.

"Ugh." I pull the blankets over my head. I haven't even started on this dumb retreat website yet, which makes it even harder. Back in high school and college, when I still used to think I would someday write high fantasy novels for a living, a blank first page was my biggest enemy.

But I know all I need to do is just get started. It's like opening a brand-new bag of chips and trying to have just one. Once you have a taste, it's like you just can't stop. Writing is a

bit similar. And it was so easy for me back then—as effortless as scarfing down an entire bag of BBQ chips.

These days, it's not the same. At all. I don't know if it's because of the anxiety getting worse or just all the head trash of being an adult with more experience that's getting in my way.

Regardless, the last thing I feel like doing is getting out of bed and starting this website. But if I don't want to be homeless by the end of the month, I don't really have a choice.

I throw the fluffy blanket away from my face and sit up, blinded by the sun that's creeping from outside. At least I can't claim I have an uninspiring setting. Apart from attending the actual Panchakarma retreat, I don't think I could have found a better place to write from.

My feet hit the ground and I'm relieved to feel the soft heat of the floor. It's going to be a warm day, at least.

In a post-sleep daze, I go through the motions as I prepare my coffee and get dressed. Well, calling it 'getting dressed' is a bit of a stretch—I just throw on some loose satin shorts and a T-shirt that looks somewhere between real clothes and pyjamas. Fuck the bra. But that's better than wearing my skimpy silk bathrobe outside.

It's a cloudless sky, and the sun is rising straight in front of the cabin, right above the ocean. It's a beautiful sight. And even though it's not practical, I set up my workstation right on the deck. The triangle top of the cabin will probably cast a shadow once the sun is higher up at noon, but for now, I have to put on my crappy old pair of sunglasses to shield myself.

But it's 100 percent worth it. I pick from one of the two

comfy lounge chairs on the deck as my battle station, prop my coffee—black, like my soul—down next to it on the deck, and start soaking it all in. The salty air. The sun. The sound of the waves.

Aww, yes.

I immediately feel myself calming down. Yup, this was the right move after all.

The first sip of my coffee cements this feeling of serenity. These moments don't come often, and they seem to require an almost impossible series of circumstances to trigger complete peace in myself like this. That's why, when they come, I soak them in with every ounce of my being.

I take in one final breath before I open my laptop and set it up on my lap. *All right*, I think to myself. *Let's get into it.*

I already did the easy part: the research phase. This involved interviewing members of the company's team, getting to understand how the retreat works, scouring through existing reviews of the experience online, stalking their competitors to see what's lacking in the space, and listening to an unholy number of podcasts and YouTube videos about the experience of Panchakarma itself. With this amount of research, it's usually easier to work from my overcrowded two-screen setup I have on my desk at home, so I don't have to switch from tab to tab as often. But the sacrifice of having a single screen on my laptop is made worth it by the setting I've immersed myself in.

I wonder what Logan's up to this morning, I think before I can stop myself. A tingling sensation fills my lower belly, and I frown. *No. Think about Logan and how ridiculously attracted I am to him later. Now?* Focus.

I end up spending the first thirty minutes setting up the document with placeholder text instead of *actually* writing anything—my favourite way to procrastinate. But at least I won't start off with a blank page—never a blank page.

Every word feels like pulling teeth out. In between a quick sandwich for lunch and one short walk down the pebbly beach, I manage to crank out a draft of the home page, and when I look back out at the sun and see how much time has passed, I gasp. *Damn.*

And when I read back what I wrote? *Damn, damn, damn.* This is shit.

For my usual standards, the copy I just wrote for this website's home page is ... okay. It's not too far off from the style some of their competitors have. But their team doesn't want 'okay.' Leslie, my main point of contact, told me the website must be 'emotive and take the reader through a transformative experience.'

And what I've written is far, far, *far* from that.

Ugh. This is going to be a long road.

Before I know it, the sun is setting already, and I've barely gotten anything of substance done. I know I have an entire month, but I had hoped I'd be able to get at least *one* section of *one* page right today. But I'm not there yet.

As I scarf down another pitiful sandwich for dinner, I think back to Logan's invitation. It makes sense, in a way. After all, I did come here for a change in scenery. Even though the view from my cabin is absolutely beautiful, I won't find much inspiration from staying in one place. I never have.

And I can't lie to myself—the idea of spending more time with Logan excites me in more ways than one. I'm no longer sure if he's forgiven me for the way our friendship ended, or if he has just stuffed it in the back of his mind and buried it underneath some other junk he hasn't processed—like any typical adult.

But I do know one thing—that he does seem to genuinely want to spend time with me.

A memory bursts through my mind:

His hips against mine. Hot breath against my neck.

I push it away as quickly as it came. Just a quick moment of it has made my cheeks flush red.

I realize he may have been expecting me to drop in today to talk more in detail about those outings he invited me on, but I got lost so deeply in my work that I didn't see the time go by. And now I don't know if Logan is the type of person who finds it okay to get a visit from someone at 8 p.m.

Because I have no idea who Logan is anymore. We've been apart for longer than we were alive when we last saw each other. Yes, I did get a first impression, and a lot of what I glimpsed from yesterday seems to be somewhat similar to the boy I once knew.

But we've both grown up. We're not even baby adults anymore; we're grade-A adults. At least, we're supposed to be.

There's a pang in my heart at the thought of that. My thirtieth birthday is looming, but I try not to think about it. Age is just a number, right?

I finish my sandwich and decide to go looking for Logan anyway when I realize I don't even know where he lives. I've only ever seen him in the lobby of the main lodge. There's a good chance he lives somewhere on the resort's property, but even if that's the case, I wouldn't know where to look. We should have exchanged numbers yesterday, but I never think about that sort of thing.

Maybe he's still working in the lobby at this hour, too. Might as well get some exercise in and walk there.

I go back inside, grab a loose knitted cardigan to protect myself from the oncoming chill of the evening sea breeze, and make my way toward the main lobby on foot. At the cabin left of mine, the two ladies who were at the patio last night are sitting around a large bonfire, each deeply engrossed in her own book. I find them brave to be reading when there's hardly any sun left.

They're not the only people at the resort who thought of bonfires, either. At least one out of two cabins I walk across has an active firepit. Must be good at keeping the mosquitos at bay.

I finally make it to the main lodge, but no luck. The lady working there tells me Logan is off this evening, so I'm back to square one.

I can't help but feel deeply disappointed, even though I knew the chances of finding him were slim. At that moment, I realize how much I need this right now. How much I need a friend like Logan.

It's not that I have no friends. Sophie and I have been thick as thieves ever since I moved to Montreal after leaving Red Lake behind with my family. In fact, she's the only one who stuck with me while everyone else called me a weirdo.

She may not understand why I don't feel comfortable around other people—because *she* definitely does—or why I love books and video games so much—because she doesn't—but she has always been there for me, especially recently with the breakup.

That being said, it's not the same as it used to be. And of course it isn't. I wouldn't expect Sophie to always be hanging out with me now that she's a mom to two beautiful little girls. But even if I don't expect it, part of me still needs it.

And even if I put that part of it aside ... There's an indescribable quality that I never shared in my friendship with Sophie. I don't know if it's because Logan and I met when we were younger, or if there's a deeper connection between the two of us, but the truth is that no one, not even Sophie, ever truly understood me the way Logan once did.

For instance, Sophie never understood why I wouldn't attend our high school graduation party. She begged and pleaded for me to go, and no matter how many times I explained it to her, she never got it.

She wasn't there when I watched the clock tick by and slowly realized that no one except my best friend was going to show up to my seventh-grade graduation party, which also happened to double as a goodbye party.

That's why Sophie ended up going to our high school graduation party with a few of her other friends—the ones who didn't like me—while I stayed home in my PJs watching *Kill Bill* with my dad. Not that I ever held it against her. I wouldn't have wanted her to miss it for anything in the world. There was just no way I could have joined her.

I snap out of my reverie and realize I've accidentally made my way to the coast some ways away from my cabin. There's a wooden bench looking out towards the ocean. Like the area near my cabin, the rocky beach is about five feet down a short cliff. And like yesterday, the fog has started creeping in.

Why not? I sit on the bench, seeing no reason to go back to my cabin right away. Might as well take in the evening breeze and drown my disappointment with the sound of the waves crashing against the rocks.

Every time a particularly large wave crashes against the pebbly beach and drags back out, I'm met with a satisfying rolling sound as the water scurries back to the ocean through thousands of stones. It's not enough to fix all my problems, but it's enough to soothe me for a moment.

I close my eyes and focus on the sound. The *'shhh'* of the incoming wave … the crash … that moment of silence … and the slithering against the rocks. It's such a simple detail, but it grounds me in the moment, easing some tension from my body.

Right then and there, I decide to make this my end-of-day ritual. A gift to myself. A moment of reprieve.

My thoughts go back to that failed graduation party. I don't like to think about that too much, but now that I've circled around it, I can't help but dive into that can of worms. The logic for planning the party in the first place was to give me the eighth-grade graduation I'd never have, since I was moving back to the province of Quebec. We spent several evenings cozied up in Logan's room, scrapbooking ideas together. But my favourite moments had to be when his mom,

Carol, would interrupt our work to grab us for a game of Uno. Which I almost always lost.

I wish I could say I wasn't still bitter about everyone in our class ghosting that party. But the truth is, I am. Why, though? I don't see a logical reason to care what a bunch of kids thought of me seventeen years ago. But I can't help it.

I look out at the ocean before me and take a deep breath, making a focused effort to relax my shoulders. The bitterness in my heart eases.

A sudden voice behind me makes me jump: "Mind if I join you?"

"Geez," I reply, meeting Logan's gaze with one hand on my chest. "I didn't hear you coming at all." He's standing behind the bench with one hand leaning against the top of it, looking amused.

"You're jumpier than before." Back during the days of our friendship, I was already a jumpy little thing. But it got worse when the panic attacks and the anxiety came. Makes sense, in a way. I'm always on edge, as if I'm waiting for the next thing in my life to attack me out of nowhere.

"Yeah." I fiddle with my hair. "But yes, please join me."

He nods and sits on the bench, leaning forward against his knees. "This is my favourite spot in the entire resort," he says. "There's always people here at sunset and sunrise. But I like to come here when it's dark out, like this." He gestures to the night sky around us.

"Yeah, I can see why this would be your favourite." It makes me a little giddy to know his favourite spot is the same as mine—and that he even shares the same ritual I wanted to start.

"So," he starts, shooting me a sly smile, "how did your writing go today?"

"Eh. It was okay." I sigh. "But you were right. I could use a little inspiration."

"Of course I was right." He winks. I pretend not to notice how my stomach somersaults in response. "You'll figure it out. Unless you got dumb over the last seventeen years. Did you get dumb, Avery?"

"Absolutely. Without you as a friend, my brain rotted away, and now only desperate people hire me." He chuckles, and so do I. "You obviously stayed smart, otherwise you wouldn't have built yourself an epic programming career."

He looks away towards the ocean. "You'd be surprised. I've worked with my fair share of idiots. And working in startups isn't as epic as it's made out to be."

There's a hint of hesitation in his voice, like he wants to say more but won't. I'm not sure what he's insinuating here.

I'm reminded of everything I *don't* know about him. There's so much of it. So much I want to know. "So how was it really? And how was it living in San Francisco?"

"It was a shock for sure. You go from a place like Red Lake to Toronto for college, which is already a big jump … but it's nothing compared to San Francisco." His eyebrows shoot up, as if to emphasize this fact. "It took a while for me to find my footing there." He chuckles. "Getting around in that place is a complete nightmare. And the gunshots took a while to get used to. Honestly, I still wasn't used to it after all those years."

"Damn." Living in Montreal, I'm accustomed to the big city—by Canadian standards. But I know American cities are another ballpark entirely. I'm suddenly hit by a pang of longing to hold Logan's hand. To tell him he did good. That he's been brave.

But I won't go there. So I settle for a sympathetic smile. "Is that why you needed a change of scenery, then?"

He nods. "Yeah, you could say that." His answer elicits more curiosity than anything else.

If that was truly why he came here, he wouldn't have said it like that. And it doesn't answer the question of why he would stop doing what he loves—and take the huge pay cut—to work in hospitality for an entire summer. Family business or not, if he has changed as little as I think, this type of public-facing job is a nightmare come true for him. In that way, we're exactly the same.

"So why not ask your boss to work remotely for the summer, then? Why work here?" I immediately realize how judgy it sounds and want to fix it right away. "Not that I'm judging, though. It's just that, I remember how much you were scared of eventually getting your first job because all there was in Red Lake for teens was customer-facing … and now here you are."

I can see right away that I've said the wrong thing. His entire body stiffens, and it looks like he has stopped breathing. He's staring out at the ocean, and I can't read what's going on in his eyes.

"I didn't mean to pry," I say, hoping this brings us back to our previous camaraderie. "You don't have to answer that if you don't want to."

He breaks his focused stare towards the water and blinks quickly. "Oh. Yeah. Sorry, I just got distracted in my thoughts a little bit." He shoots me a look and smiles. "I guess I wanted to try it out. Call it a sabbatical or whatever." But there's something off about his tone, and I can tell that's not the complete truth.

"And how has it been?"

He shrugs. "Eh. Most people don't suck. But … still."

That isn't even an attempt at an answer. Yet, I don't push it. What right do I have? I was the one who catapulted my way out of his life. And now, seventeen years later, I can't just waltz back in and expect him to lay his entire heart out for me on a silver platter. That's not how it works.

Baby steps. For now, I'll take what I can get.

It takes all of my willpower not to scooch up against him and squeeze him tight. Because I can tell, just from the way his gaze has wandered again, that whatever he's not telling me is hurting him. And I can't stand to see him hurt like this.

Even if he won't show me.

Logan never wore his emotions on his sleeve. Even when we were thick as thieves, I never once saw him cry, apart from when his dog died. Not even as eight-year-olds. Not even that time a bully had shoved him so hard against the swing poles that he wore dark bruises for weeks. While I was a constant emotional mess who couldn't hold anything back, he processed what he went through in silence. And if he cried, he sure as hell didn't show anyone. Even me, despite how close we had been. It's like he never wanted to be a burden on me or his mom.

We were basically all he had.

But he still had little tells that something was off, even though he would rarely admit it. The way his head slouched down just a bit. The slight shift in his eyebrows. And that quality in his eyes that's so difficult to describe … the kind of thing you only notice when you've known someone so deeply that you feel like you can see right down to their soul.

I'm snapped out of my thoughts when he sits down on the bench next to me. He's close enough that I feel the warmth emanating from his skin. I resist the urge to close the few inches of space that are left between us.

"You know," I start, planting my hands firmly on my thighs so they don't wander somewhere they shouldn't go, "if you were looking to switch things up, I don't know if you're still into video games, but …"

He raises one eyebrow. "But what?"

"Why not do that? Go into game development, I mean." To me, it makes much more sense to try something that could reignite this passion. That would certainly switch things up. "You'd be programming and working on games. I can't see how that could go wrong."

Logan sighs. He's still staring out at the ocean, looking pensive. "It's not that simple, Avery."

"How so?"

"Game dev is a beast on its own, and the industry is …" His voice trails off. "Anyway." He gives me a smile before turning back to the ocean. "I'm happy to be here right now."

He doesn't say the words, but by the way he looks at me,

I can feel them hanging in the air between us:

With you.

I hold my breath. Before I can resist the urge to say it, because it's none of my business, I ask: "So then, did you come here alone, or are you doing a long-distance thing, or …"

Smooth, Avery. Real smooth.

He looks at me, frowning with one raised eyebrow. "Huh?"

"I mean …" I twist my fingers together. I got myself into this. I can't blame him for making me say it out loud. "I already told you I just got dumped. So I was wondering if you've been any luckier with these things."

"Oh." He starts chewing the inside of his cheek. "I wouldn't really say lucky, no."

"No?" I'm feeling a bit conflicted. This should make me upset for him. It only makes sense that I would want him to be lucky in that department. Luckier than me, at least. So why am I feeling relieved?

He looks away. "Work keeps me busy a ton. And, I mean, I've had a few … flings, here and there. But nothing serious, ever."

Ever?

"Is that something you're looking for?" I feel the urge to wrap my arms around him to give him some comfort. But I stay seated exactly where I am.

"Yes and no." He steals one glance at me before looking away again. "I'd be willing to fight for it with the right person. But up until now, that hasn't happened." My heart flutters at those words. "I'm okay with that, though."

A weight lifts from my chest. Knowing that he's okay with that, and that he hasn't been heartbroken like I am … it's a relief.

"What?" He's looking at me with a puzzled expression. I must have sighed more loudly than I intended.

I don't see any use in lying my way out of this one. "I guess I'm just happy to know there isn't a woman out there who tore your heart out and set it on fire before running away." Then I look up at the sky to watch the stars so I can avoid his gaze.

"Is that what happened to you?"

I think of Jasper. The memory of his stupid face still burns like a knife in my heart. Five years. I woke up next to this man for half a decade, thinking that would be the rest of my life. Every groove I had with him in my life slowly deepened over time, and now I have no idea how to break out of them. I don't know how I'll ever go back to that stupid apartment.

"You could say that."

I wait for him to ask a follow-up question, but he doesn't. He simply looks at me, without any pressure in his eyes. He's offering to listen.

Before I can stop myself, words start spilling out of my mouth. "We were together for five years, sharing an apartment, sharing basically everything, and then one morning before he's supposed to go to Italy with his brother, he decides he's done. Just … done. No explanation. And that was it." My chest tightens at the memory. My throat feels dry.

"Wait …" Logan shifts to face me fully. "You guys talked it out later, right?"

I look down at my feet swinging from the bench. "No."

"You're serious?"

"Yes."

"What an absolute asshole." His voice is loud, though I can hear him trying to restrain himself. "The coward. I can't believe he would do that to you."

"He wasn't an asshole before," I say, my voice barely louder than a whisper.

"No, that's not possible, Avery," he continues, the anger resonating in his voice. I take one look at his face and get a glimpse of anger I've rarely ever seen—not even when the bullies took shots at him.

That's when I realize: he isn't pissed because someone hurt *him*. He's pissed because someone hurt *me*.

"You don't just become an asshole overnight. He showed you who he really was when he did that. And who he is just so happens to be a selfish coward."

"You don't even know him," I argue.

"I don't need to." The golden flecks in his hazel eyes are burning in the moonlight. "That act alone speaks volumes about his character. You didn't deserve that, Avery."

Didn't I? I don't know. I've been racking my brain over what could have driven him to do this, and every time I do, I come to the same conclusion. Five years with me was more than enough.

But I don't want to think about that now. Right now, I just want to think about the way Logan is defending me. Even if he's wrong, he's helping me feel a little bit less like discarded trash.

"Thank you." I keep my voice soft so it doesn't crack.

"No need to thank me." He turns back around, his body starting to calm down from the anger. "It's just logic. And he's a fool."

I laugh, thinking to myself that right now, my life doesn't feel *that* bad.

—

It's almost 10 p.m. by the time I walk back inside my cabin. Logan headed back to his place pretty much at the same time as I did, but not before inviting me to our first outing for tomorrow. He hasn't settled on what we'll do yet, but he'll have the entire day to decide since we're meeting for dinner.

And this time, we exchanged phone numbers.

I crash face-first into the cushy king-sized bed and sigh. I wish I could fast-forward through the day of gruelling writing and skip straight to dinner with Logan. Spending time with him makes me almost feel human again. It's not like I'm completely over this slump or whatever this is, but almost.

My thoughts trail to Dad, and my heart sinks. I roll on my back and pull out my phone, already knowing I won't find any notifications from him. But I need to check anyway.

Nope. Nothing except the last message I sent him, still left unread.

Without too much thought, I begin typing a new message.

I wish you could meet the person Logan became. He feels exactly the same, yet different. Good different. But knowing how you can read people, maybe you'd be able to tell what's going on with him. I don't know what it is. And I don't know if I should pry.

I also wish you could tell me what's going on with me. You know what I mean. I don't know how you do it, but you always seem to be a step ahead of me. I bet you would have known Jasper was about to leave me, even though it came out of nowhere for me.

I need some direction, Dad. I don't know what's going on with you, and I hope you're okay… but I need a dad right now, and I just wish you'd respond. Even just for a minute. Everything feels fucked and I need one person to tell it like it is to me and no one knows how to do that except you.

Why won't you let me help?

I hit send, and the tears start falling.

Chapter 7

pull the rod back with a violent twist and feel resistance. *Gotcha.* But as soon as I start reeling the line back in, it goes slack again.

Ugh. This day hadn't gone much better than yesterday, and even my fishing stinks. It seemed like I'd just woken up and started writing just five minutes ago, but when I noticed I'd been up for hours, I knew I had to take a break. That's when I headed to a rocky corner of the coast to fish. I'd seen other people fishing here from the cliff by my cabin, and it turns out there's a small shack that rents out gear.

Thing is, I've never fished in the sea. This is nothing like lake fishing. No luck so far.

To make matters worse, I was forced to share my shitty writing progress with Leslie this morning. The first draft of the home page was due, and I didn't have a choice. The Zoom call I had with her to hear her thoughts felt like pulling teeth.

"It's missing the … emotional punch," she told me. "The magic. We want people to go through an entire transformation as they're reading the website—do you get me?"

I got her. I just don't know how to make it happen.

I sigh and finish reeling the line in. This is probably it for today. While I'm enjoying having my bare feet on the rocks and the water lapping at my toes, I could do without the fishing part. After all, I always preferred the 'being on a boat' part of fishing more than the actual fishing itself.

That, and spending time with Dad.

Our quiet memories on the lake with a fishing rod in our hands are some of my favourite memories with Dad. We both felt uncomfortable with small talk, so neither of us felt forced to say something just to fill the silence. We could spend hours at a time just listening to the quiet lap of the water against the boat in those early hours of the morning.

When one of us did speak, it was to say something real. Like when he'd asked me how I was doing in school, not as a formality, but because he actually wanted to know, deep down, how I was getting along. And whenever I let him know it wasn't going as well as I wanted, he always had words of encouragement for me. It's like he always knew what to say.

Those fishing trips became less and less frequent when we moved back from Red Lake to Montreal. Not only were Dad's work trips longer, but we also had to go out of our way to find a good spot away from the city. Still, it didn't stop me from asking. And when I asked, we'd go.

But as time went on, Dad spent more and more time in the evenings locked up in my parents' room. Sometimes, I'd see him for dinner, and that was it. And I could see what it did to Mom, too. She didn't let it show, but I could tell she was lonely. Even though I couldn't bring myself to care for them, I'd spend time curled up on the couch next to her as she caught up with her franco TV dramas and folded laundry. Mom didn't fare well alone.

I head back to the cabin and begrudgingly get back into writing again. Before I know it, a knock on the door jolts me from my work. I glance at the clock—6 p.m. My mood immediately shifts from sour to elated.

This has to be Logan.

I immediately jump to my feet, then cringe as I gaze down at myself, which is ridiculous if I think about it. Logan and I basically grew up together. He saw me in way worse than these sweatshorts and ripped T-shirt. So why is this suddenly making me self-conscious?

I take a deep breath and head to the door, swinging it open with a grin.

"Hey," Logan says casually as he steps inside, his eyes scanning my outfit. "New fashion statement?"

I roll my eyes but can't help the laugh that bubbles out of me. "Shut up. This is every copywriter's work uniform."

Logan chuckles as he drops himself into one of the two cushy chairs at the table. "Right. Makes sense. So how's the writing going?"

I groan as I imitate him and fall back into my own chair—the same one I've practically spent all day in, except for that quick fishing stint. "I'm about ready to throw my computer out the window."

Logan winces. "That bad, huh?"

I nod, throwing my head back with a sigh. "I don't know what's wrong with me. Every time I start to write, it just feels like … I don't know, like I'm completely empty of anything."

Logan's eyes soften and he grabs my hand, squeezing it lightly. The warmth of his skin sends a soft tingle through my body. My heart skips a beat and I'm filled with a newfound rush, like I've swallowed a whole colony of bees. It's comforting yet unsettling at the same time—a strange combination that has me wanting more, even if I don't know why.

"That's exactly why you need these outings with me," he says softly. "You need to get out of your head and get away from the computer for a while. You can't spend all your time in front of it; you need to take a break every now and then."

I freeze, mesmerized by his warm gaze. His words feel like a revelation. He's right—I'm not doing myself any favours if I stay cooped up in this room all day, every day. Even if I take a break or two, I need to widen my horizons a bit more to get this inspiration flowing. That's why I agreed to his idea in the first place.

Well, that and the fact that I absolutely want to spend more time with him while I'm here.

Logan must sense the shift in my mood because he squeezes my hand again before releasing it and giving me a small smile. My breath hitches.

"So, are you ready for our first outing?" he asks, raising an eyebrow at me expectantly.

My heart flutters as I nod, feeling my face crack into a wide grin. Then I remember what I look like, and I gaze back down at myself. "Umm … I'm gonna need a minute."

"Sure." He laughs, then gets up from the chair. "I'll wait outside." As he's just about to shut the door, he peeks his head back inside to tell me: "By the way, you look great. I was just kidding earlier, you know that, right?" And before I can respond, he shuts the door, leaving me alone in my cabin.

My cheeks flush, and a warmth spreads through my chest. I take a few deep breaths, trying to calm my racing heart. Then, with a newfound energy, I hurry up to get ready, throwing on whatever I can find and trying my best with my messy hair.

I slip on an old pair of sneakers and some jeans that are slightly too long, but comfortable enough that they don't drag on the ground. I've pretty much just brought ratty T-shirts and tank tops with me, but I manage to find a button-up short-sleeved shirt that isn't completely off-putting. Finally, I brush some mascara over my eyes—just enough to make them stand out—and tie my hair up into a messy-but-cute bun before grabbing my purse and heading outside.

I open the door to see Logan staring out at the ocean. He turns at the sound, his face brightening when he sees me.

He doesn't say anything, but he certainly looks stunned. It's only when I look at him funny that he straightens his face. I attempt to do the same.

"We can head to the lodge—my car's parked there," he tells me as he starts walking. I follow, giving one quick glance back at the ocean. I can't help but wonder what he was thinking about before I came out of the cabin.

The two of us used to be perfectly acquainted with

watching the other live in their little bubble like this. We used to spend hours side by side, quietly relaxing in his room or under a tree somewhere; I'd be writing in my notebook while he played on his Gameboy or learned how to code on his laptop. And he knew for a fact that when I had my focused face on, I was not to be disturbed. He never did. Me? Most of the time, I left him alone. But sometimes, I'd tease him and tell him to work on his code instead of playing on his Gameboy.

Soon, we make it to the lodge, and Logan gestures to a black sedan. He makes his way to the driver's seat.

"So, where are we headed?" I ask as I climb into the car with him. The inside smells nice, which is a change from the constant sweaty smell I had to endure in Jasper's car. Until now, I'd believed all guys had messy cars by default. Maybe I'm wrong; maybe not all guys leave their gym equipment in their car overnight because they can't be bothered to carry it back and forth from the apartment.

It doesn't just smell nice, though. The scent is identical to what I picked up when I had my face against him the other day after my panic attack. I try to think of literally anything else because it's tantalizing.

Logan turns the key in the ignition, then flashes me a mischievous grin.

"We're heading to my favourite eatery," he explains as he pulls away from the curb. "It's usually missed by tourists, but all the locals hang there."

"Oh, so you're a local already, huh? You mean you actually socialize?"

He goes red and chuckles. "I guess so. I'm not sure why. I just feel at ease there."

We drive for a while before I see what looks like an old house with a sign that reads, 'The Coastal Kitchen.' Logan parks on the street and we make our way inside as my stomach is doing flips.

Is this a date? Nah, it's probably not a date.

So why do I feel like I'm on one?

The overwhelming scent of grilled seafood and delicious baked goods fills the air as we walk in. It's clear right from my first impression that this restaurant isn't fancy at all but cozy and warm instead.

The warm lighting of the restaurant casts shadows on the brick walls, while sunbeams peek through the windows, illuminating a few tables here and there. A small bar lined with stools sits in the corner next to a worn piano. There's the gentle crackling of a fire in the corner, which immediately makes me nostalgic for the evenings spent by the bonfire over the summer with Logan. Soft conversations and laughter rising from the tables make the air feel almost alive.

I *love* it.

Logan leads me to a booth in the corner and we sit down. A short but stout waitress in her fifties comes over and hands us two menus. Instinctively, I put on my social mask and try to sit up straighter.

The waitress winks at Logan. "Don't tell me you are *finally* bringing a date here!" she exclaims, looking straight at me. My face flushes.

Logan goes beet-red. We probably match. "Oh, no,

no, this is Avery, an old friend of mine," he replies quickly. Quickly enough that he almost makes it sound like this being a date would be the worst thing on the planet.

I deflate a bit at his tone. Not that I was absolutely expecting this to be a date, but it does make me feel weird to hear him respond so quickly.

Ugh. I need to get it together. I'm not even supposed to be dating, anyway. Seeing as I can't write properly, I'm clearly not over my breakup. The last thing I should do is rope someone as sweet as Logan into my mess.

"Well, a friend of Logan's is a friend of ours here," the waitress responds with another wink. With her dimples and wide smile, she reminds me of the typical, kind aunt that would squeeze your cheeks if you let her get close enough.

I smile awkwardly and try to ignore my heart hammering against my ribcage. "Hehe, hi."

Dread crawls through my arms all the way to my fingers. What was that?

"I'll let ya take a look, then, honey," she responds, ignoring my weird reply. Before I know it, she's gone from our table, and I shake off this anxious energy.

Logan explains: "I always order the same thing. And if you're still a fan of shrimp like you used to be, I highly advise you to do the same."

"Oh, yeah? What is it?"

He nods, his eyes lighting up as he talks about the food. "The shrimp pesto pasta. Seriously, it's ridiculous how good it is. You won't regret it."

I nod, feeling relieved that I don't have to spend too

much time thinking about what to order. I'm already nervous enough as it is, which feels kind of ridiculous. It's true that I haven't been out in a while—not since the breakup—but this feels like next-level caveman behaviour. "Okay, then, shrimp pesto pasta it is." I set down my menu, not even bothering to look through the rest.

It's quiet between us for a moment before Logan speaks up again. "So, I've been wondering about something," he says hesitantly. "I can't say I'm completely surprised to know you're a copywriter. But I have to ask—why copy and not stories?"

I freeze, caught off guard by the question. My heart races in my chest as I try to figure out how to answer him without sounding like a complete failure.

"Oh, you know," I start, then let my sentence trail off.

He looks at me, puzzled. "Uh, not really, no. You were always the writer. I was the logical one. So I have no idea about anything."

How do I tell him the truth without sounding completely materialistic? It's not like I didn't try. I don't even remember how many manuscripts I came up with and sent over to publishers, only to hear crickets back. And even when I tried to handle publishing myself, nothing came of it.

There's a chance I could have persevered if I wanted to. But hopes don't pay the bills. Copywriting does.

I shrug and look down at the menu, fiddling with it to occupy my hands. "Well, I figured I might as well get paid for writing if no one wants to read my fiction, you know?"

Logan nods slowly, but I can tell he isn't completely convinced by my answer. "I get it. It's too bad, though. I remember the stories you used to tell me when we were kids. They always made me laugh, but in a good way, you know." His eyes go bright. "But mostly, I remember how you looked when you were writing. Your face would completely change. It was like you were gone in another world entirely. That's one of the things that I loved the most about you."

My breath catches in my throat. It's difficult to imagine we spent so long apart when we had been so close. Because we were that close. We did love each other, as friends do. As families do.

At least, that's what I try to tell myself. But the memory of his body against mine in the dark says otherwise. The sound of his heartbeat against my ear, the feel of his chest, the warmth of—

Cut it out, Avery.

"Since I still write, I guess I've made it more than most," I continue. "I mean, I could be stuck in some dead-end job typing up reports or whatever. But I actually get to use my creativity and write stuff. So it's not all bad."

"You're the one who knows yourself best." Logan shrugs. "All I know is, you seem to be struggling a ton with this project. Not that it's not okay or anything. Obviously, you can't be on your A-game all the time."

"Yeah, I—"

"So, what will it be, honey?" I almost have a heart attack when the waitress creeps back up on us. I was so caught up in our conversation that I didn't notice her at all.

"We'll both have the shrimp pesto pasta," Logan tells her.

"You got it, then. Anything to drink?"

Shoot. I hadn't even thought about looking at the drinks. Logan looks at me, seeming like he's detecting my nerves.

"Uh," I stammer before I frantically grab the menu. "Um, uh … this." I point at something called Wicked Minx Sour. "Yeah, this."

"You sure? You don't need more time?"

"Yeah, yeah, I want this."

She gives me a side-eye, which seems to be more out of concern than judgement. "Alrighty, then. And for you, the usual?"

Logan nods. "Yup, thanks, Judith." When she's gone, Logan turns his attention to me again. "Hey, you okay?"

Seventeen years apart and he still knows how to read me so easily. I wring my hands together under the table. "Sure. I'm just …" I pause. "A little nervous, I guess."

I'm never this upfront about my social anxiety. I always expect people to question me or ask me why or look at me weird. In the few times I've mentioned being nervous in a situation where most people aren't, I've gotten judgy looks. So now, I just bite my tongue.

But Logan doesn't give me a weird look. Instead, he shoots me a sympathetic smile. And he waits patiently for me to continue if I need to.

It warms my heart. But it also feels a bit disorienting. I'm used to people speaking over me, or at least starting to talk as soon as I take a moment to breathe. So it takes me a moment to get my bearings and keep speaking.

"Social stuff is kind of hard for me." I keep wringing my hands and avert my eyes from his attentive gaze. "You know about the panic attacks. But talking to people I don't know … it doesn't necessarily give me a panic attack every time. It's more like … it's…"

I clench my jaw in frustration. If I were writing this, it would be easy, but it's so difficult to find the right words when I'm speaking out loud. "It's like every time I need to talk to someone who doesn't deeply, truly know me—and there aren't a lot of these people—it's like someone has thrown a weighted blanket over me, but not a good kind, like a way too heavy kind, and everything is harder because I have to put on this mask. And at the same time, it's like my mind becomes all foggy and I can't think straight, so whatever I say comes out as gibberish."

I stop to take a breath, then finally look into Logan's eyes. "And … I deal with it. I go to therapy. All the stuff you're supposed to do. But for some reason this entire year, it feels like it's gotten worse, and now this anxiety is creeping into my creative work, and then I got dumped on top of everything else, plus my dad—" I stop mid-sentence.

Logan cocks his head sideways. "What about your dad?"

Dread crawls through my chest like vines. This is one part of my life I'm not ready to share with anyone yet. Not even my former best friend. "Oh, he's just, I don't know … but anyway, like I said, I manage. It's not as bad as it seems." Except it is.

Before Logan can reply, Judith is back with our drinks. I nearly snatch it from her before she can place it on the table. I take a big sip from the pink straw. It's good.

Logan takes a sip of his own beer, then places his forearms on the table to lean against it. "You should have told me before. We could have gone to an activity with fewer people."

"No, I actually like going out where there's people," I stammer. "And that's why I deal with it. Because I need that social interaction. I like going out and feeling the hum of people. It's just … I need to recover after, if that makes sense."

If it was so simple as avoiding social interactions, I'd just become a hermit and move as far away from the city as possible. But I'd get lonely too quickly. "Plus, this place is pretty cool. It's exactly the kind of spot I'd choose if I were on my own."

Logan's shoulders seem to relax. He looks relieved. "Okay. That's good to know. But you can tell me if it's becoming too much and then we can leave. I'm okay with that."

"Okay."

"And you know you don't have to act like anyone but yourself around me," he reminds me with a crooked smile.

I look down shyly. "I know."

Before either of us can say anything else, an old man walking by our booth stops with a big smile.

"Logan!" the man exclaims right before giving Logan a big tap on the shoulder. "I didn't even know you were here! How come we haven't heard you at the piano yet?"

Logan's cheeks go red. "Oh, well, I'm with someone, so I didn't think to—"

"Wait," I interrupt, suddenly feeling giddy. "You play piano?" This is new. Back when we were kids, doing anything creative for him felt like pulling teeth. And he sang like a strangled cat.

Although, playing an instrument can also be a technical

feat, so I shouldn't be surprised at what he's capable of.

The old man beams and slaps his hands down on the table, making me jump. "Oh, does he ever! He always plays for us folks here. Dontcha, Logan?"

A lady two tables across from our booth joins the conversation:

"Yes, go play! I've been waiting for you to go! Don't disappoint us!"

"How are you shy all of a sudden?" the old man asks Logan, whose face looks like it's going to spontaneously combust. "Is it because of this beautiful little lady here?" Now it's my turn to blush. "Are we interrupting a date?"

"Huh? No, no," Logan reassures the old man before standing from the booth. He shoots me an uncertain smile. "Yeah, I play. Do you mind if I go do a song or two to appease these guys?"

Trying to ignore my self-consciousness from the old man's comments, I nod with enthusiasm. "Absolutely not, I don't mind. I can't wait to hear you play. Go, go." I shoo him off with my hands and give him a toothy grin.

Satisfied he got my permission, Logan makes his way to the piano by the bar. It's an old, rustic thing that's probably been here as long as this building, but it's part of what makes this place so cozy. I don't take my eyes off him for a second while he sits at the bench, stretches his fingers a bit, and finally begins to play.

When I recognize the opening notes of *All of Me* by John Legend, my entire body freezes with shock. My favourite song. This can't be a coincidence, can it? I try to remember if I mentioned this was my favourite song during any of our conversations over the past few days ... but I can't recall mentioning it at all.

The notes are crystal clear, perfectly executed, and the restaurant has gone still. I'm not the only one enthralled by the music, but I think I'm the only one who cannot—even for a single microsecond—look away from Logan as his fingers dance on the keyboard with grace.

There's something unfurling in my chest, like a small flower blooming and spreading its petals against my sternum. Suddenly, there's nothing but Logan and the music, and the restaurant fades away. My vision tunnels straight into him.

His playing is beautiful. *He* is beautiful.

A wave of emotion washes through me, and I have to bite my lip to keep my eyes from watering. The last thing I want is to embarrass myself and take the attention away from him. But it's so hard not to let this wave completely overtake me. I don't think I've ever felt something quite as powerful as this.

Even though I don't want to look away, I close my eyes just for a moment. And that's when I realize it's gone.

The weight. The dread. Everything that's been pulling me down for the last several months. In that magical moment, it's all gone. All I feel is warmth, and bliss, and—

Something else that's deeply familiar yet brand new. In that moment, listening to the notes engulfing me, I'm thirteen again, buried in Logan's arms, never wanting to let go.

Too soon, the song ends and brings me back to the present moment as everyone in the restaurant claps. I shake myself off and join them enthusiastically, still not looking away from

Logan.

That's when he turns around and looks straight at me. He's absolutely beaming. My insides go fuzzy.

What is happening to me?

Chapter 8

I still haven't broken the gaze between us when the same old man who interrupted our meal exclaims:

"One more!"

Logan looks at the man, then back at me, as if asking for permission. I blink a few times, still dazed by everything that just went through my head, and then give him a nonchalant nod and mouth, "Go ahead."

Before I know it, he begins playing again, this time with Adele's *Set Fire to the Rain*. While it's not my favourite, it is another song that's dear to me, and I'm beginning to wonder if Logan has done more sleuthing on me than I first thought.

After all, if I kept up with what he's been doing all these years, wouldn't it stand to reason that he'd do the same?

But that's not what I should be thinking about. What I should be thinking about is the way his music is making me feel.

I don't dare put any words to the way my insides are turning to jelly. Because this is new. Well—*new* is one way to put it. I did feel this pull, this full-body tingle, a few other times when we were younger. One time, I'd run to his house, absolutely destroyed about the fact my dad would miss graduation. He'd held me so tight, and I'd felt it then. What I'm feeling now.

And there was graduation night.

But I can't entertain this. Logan was my best friend. That was it. Right? And he could become my best friend again if circumstances are right. I know it sounds cliché to say, but I don't have many friends, so the last thing I want is to lose him.

And even if I were to explore what I'm feeling … I don't know if I'd be ready to relocate to San Francisco to pursue anything more. I can't ask Logan to move to Montreal. His career is over there. Maybe I could move someday, but certainly not right now, especially while I'm still confused.

But those aren't the only reasons I can't entertain this thought.

I think of my dad and Jasper and feel my heart sink. For some reason, I wasn't good enough for Jasper. And even my own dad, who's supposed to be there for me when shit hits the fan … even he won't talk to his own daughter.

It's not like the rest of my life with him was different. He was always travelling for work and gone for extended periods of time—months, even. The longest I remember him being gone was four months, but two to three months wasn't uncommon. Then he'd come back for two weeks, and

I'd finally get to see him until he left again for another two months at least.

When we were living it, I at least consoled myself with the fact that he was doing this to provide for us. He did it because the job demanded it. And I believed that for a long time. But I still remember the pang of horror I felt when Mom told me the truth about his work trips.

I'd been at Mom's tiny new apartment soon after Dad had left her, sipping some tea with her at the dingy dinner table she'd gotten off Craigslist. This was a few months after the worst of the pain had ebbed through her, and I did my best to spend as much time as I could with her so she didn't have to be alone. At that point, she'd still been a bit raw about the topic of Dad.

Which is exactly why I should have avoided that topic, but somehow, there I was, talking about him.

"I still don't understand why Dad didn't complain to the company when they sent him away for so long." I'd sighed in between two sips of tea. Right away, Mom's face had shifted. I couldn't tell if the look on her face was anger, pity, or both. "What?"

"You've got it the other way around, honey." She'd huffed and looked out the window, a fire lit in her eyes. "You know the usual shifts they did here. 14-14, 7-7, 4-3, or 30-14 at worst. Do you really think they would have forced your father to leave for ninety whole days at a time and only take two weeks off in between?"

Dread had crawled through me like a viper. "What do you mean?"

She'd rolled her eyes and scoffed. "It was always him. He loves you, and I'm pretty sure he loved me, too." Her eyes had gone watery. "But I know he never felt at ease in this kind of life. This sedentary family life. It restricted him from the ability to go wherever he wanted to, because I never wanted to uproot your life every year. It's like we trapped him or choked him. So, of course, he insisted they keep him away longer so he could help out. The company was just glad they could get more man-hours out of him, and he was happy in that role. Now he's exactly where he always wanted to be."

I'm reliving the same horrible, sinking feeling as I think back to that moment of realization while Adele's haunting piano notes still ring in my ear. The overstuffed restaurant booth is about to swallow me whole.

I can't do this with Logan. Because I can't stand being not good enough for someone so important to me. Not again.

But I can behave. I've done it before. Before Jasper, there was this cute college professor I couldn't stop thinking about with the dimples of a Greek god. Completely inappropriate. And that's why I never pursued him.

So I can do this. I can do friends.

My thoughts get interrupted by another round of clapping, and I realize Logan has wrapped up the song. He gives a small wave to the restaurant patrons and staff before he heads back towards me.

"Sorry about that," he says as he slides into his side of the booth. He immediately takes a sip of his beer. "I always play for the gang when I come here, so I guess they have expectations now. Even when I'm with someone." He looks at me sheepishly.

I try to forget how mesmerized his piano skills just made me feel and take a big gulp of my drink. It's just Logan. Of course he's good at the piano. He was always the best at everything.

But I can see from the way he's looking at me that he knows something's wrong. And it doesn't take him a long time to speak up. "You sure you're okay?"

I take a deep breath, trying to make it appear normal. "Yeah, yeah! I'm just hungry. And I enjoyed your little show there." And then, because I've just got to ask and I can't help myself: "How did you know about *All of Me*?" Realizing how that sounded out loud, I immediately add, "The song, I mean. Not, like all of 'me' me." I gesture to my body to drive the point home, then internally cringe at the way I'm acting. *Shut up, Avery.*

Logan goes red again and starts chewing the inside of his cheek. Even after all this time apart, he still has the same little quirks and habits. It's the same thing as when you notice a father and son side-by-side who move in an eerily similar pattern and have nearly identical mannerisms.

"Yeah, I was wondering if I was going to get away with that," he replies, just as Judith comes swooping in with what looks like the most delicious shrimp pesto pasta I've ever laid eyes on.

"Holy …" I take it all in, staring at the plate with hunger. But then I remember not to get distracted and look back at Logan, who has the same plate set in front of him. "And nope, you're not getting away with it. Even food won't distract me from the obvious fact that you somehow know my favourite song."

He chuckles and grabs his fork to dig in. "It's funny. You still stare at food the exact same way you used to."

I point at him with my fork, feigning annoyance. "Don't you change the subject, sir!"

"Okay, okay." He takes a bite and slowly chews before continuing. He's doing it on purpose; he obviously finds this hilarious. "So, when I got the idea to take you here, I went digging a bit on Instagram and saw you mention this was your favourite song."

"Yeah. I did. In a post from, like, three years ago." I shoot him a coy smile.

"Yup. I know." He shrugs and grabs another bite. "But I was determined to figure it out."

I try not to let myself feel warm and fuzzy at the fact that he likely spent close to an hour, if not more, trying to find my favourite song just so he could perform it in front of me later. There's so much to appreciate about this man. To distract myself, I finally grab a bite of the scrumptious-looking meal right in front of me.

My eyes go wide. "Oh. My. God." I look down at my bowl, then back at Logan. "This has got to be the best shrimp dish I've ever eaten in my life."

"Didn't I tell you?" He smiles with pride. "Pretty much everything here is good, but this one tops it. And the worst thing is, tourists miss out. This place isn't by the water, and it doesn't look like much from the outside, and from what the staff here has told me, tourists who do come hardly ever try the pasta. They go for the steaks and ribs."

We keep chatting as we're each enjoying this amazing meal at the same time. The conversation comes easy, like breathing, and for this vignette of a moment, I feel how I felt when Logan played piano earlier.

Weightless. At peace. Like everything is going to be okay.

Before I know it, we've both finished our meal, Judith has whisked our plates away, and we've each got a check in front of us. But Logan frowns, then grabs Judith's wrist before she can leave.

"What's up, honey?" she asks, not at all jolted by Logan grabbing her. He really must be a regular.

"Can we actually get just one check, please?" I try to interject, but he raises his hand to interrupt me. "Don't even try. I invited you, so obviously I'm paying. Also, you don't need any more anxiety about extra bills to pay, so this is happening, and don't you dare try to fight me on this one."

I stay quiet and squeeze my lips together. He's got a point. I'm all for equality and splitting the bill. But I'm not the type of person who'll throw a hissy fit if you try to pay the bill for me, either.

I just hate how much this makes it seem even more like a date.

Because it's clearly *not* a date.

"Thank you," I reply. Then I squint my eyes at him. "But I'll get you back. Somehow. When I land my next contract or something."

"Yeah, yeah. We'll see."

We finish up and get ready to leave. But I'm not ready for

the evening to end. Evidently, neither is Logan, because as soon as we're both in his car he shoots me an intriguing look. "Wanna see something cool?"

I can't help but notice how close our faces are in this car. The air feels taut, like someone's holding an elastic around our two bodies and it's about to snap and pull us closer. I blink several times and try to get my breath in order. "Depends what it is, because it sounds like you're planning to take me to your murder spot near the woods or something."

He laughs, and his laughter infects me. "Nah, I'd never show you my murder spot. I wouldn't want you stealing it and getting us both caught with your sloppy amateur work."

My hand shoots to my chest as I feign indignation. "I'm nothing if not a pure professional! How dare you question my skills?"

"So I'm guessing it's a yes, then?" He raises his eyebrows, beckoning me to take him up on the invitation.

I don't know if I should. On the one hand, friends show friends cool secret things all the time. And I know for certain that I do want Logan as a friend again. Because now that I feel what it's like to have him back in my life, I don't ever want to go back.

On the other hand, I don't like this slippery slope. I'm afraid I'll do something I regret or give him the wrong idea. "Actually, do you mind if we drive back to the resort for tonight?" I can see his disappointment immediately. "It's not that I'm not curious about your murder spot," I say, trying to keep it light. "I'm just really tired. And I want to be able to wake up and be productive tomorrow. You know?"

He gives me a few quick nods. "Yeah, of course." He starts the car in silence.

"Maybe you can take me there for our next outing," I say to encourage him. Even though I don't want to give him the wrong idea, I also don't want him to think I don't want to spend time with him.

"That's an idea," he says, but his mood has obviously changed. Shoot. A weight presses against my chest. I hope he's not too hurt.

The drive back is relatively quiet, but I do my best to keep it light. By the time we're back at my cabin, the air feels like static. It's a good thing I said no because I'm finding it hard to keep my hands to myself.

"Good night, then," he says as I leave his car.

"Good night, Logan." I give him the best smile I can muster despite the weight in my chest. "And thank you. I had a great time. And I'm pretty sure I'm going to wake up more inspired tomorrow morning."

"That's the goal, isn't it?" He gives me a quick goodbye with his hand. "I'll see you soon, then. Sleep well, Avery."

I watch him drive away and wrap my arms around myself, aware of the sudden chill of the evening air. I'm making the right choice. I can make a friend, get inspired, finish this project, and then focus on working on myself to get over this damn existential crisis.

Easy peasy.

Chapter 9

A few days later, I've gotten some progress done on the website, but the sweltering heat is begging me to go for a dip.

I head down the rocky path to the beach, my flip-flops slapping against the weathered stones. The wind whips my hair as I emerge from the cliffs to the shoreline. I shrug off my coverup and wade into the foamy surf, gasping as the cold water embraces my legs.

I plunge forward, swimming with sure strokes. The waves buoy me up and send me crashing down, the rhythm of the sea. I surface, blinking salt from my eyes, feeling alive. There's nothing quite like the feeling of floating.

I want to stay in the water forever, but I suddenly glimpse a silhouette coming my way. Even though he's still far away, I recognize Logan. He's marching with a bounce in his step, looking like he's in a great mood.

My stomach does a flip as I look at him approaching. It's been a few days since our outing at the restaurant, and I haven't seen much of him since. I occasionally took breaks and walked around to stretch my legs and potentially run into him, and even went to grab a drink at the lodge a few times, but every time I came back disappointed.

We did text a bit, but he couldn't skip out early from work. I do still see him every evening at the bench, though. We sort of fell into this ritual without speaking a word about it. Every evening, I make my way to the bench facing the coast, and I'm always the first to arrive. But I never wait too long alone before Logan joins me.

We'll always chat a bit about how my writing is going, the renovations at the resort, and anything in between. But often, we'll just drift into silence and listen to the waves crash and roll through the pebbly beach below. And it feels so right.

I did try to ask why I haven't seen him around this week, but he's been squirrely about it. He keeps circling back to supply runs for the renovations without going into too much detail, so I don't push him. But the way he tenses up ever so slightly when I ask gives me the impression that there's something he's not telling me.

And that's his right. It's not like he owes me anything. I'm already lucky enough that he wants to spend time with me.

Logan is nearly at the waterline when I realize I'll have to get out of the water in my bathing suit with him here. I'm suddenly self-conscious. With me being so short, the few extra pounds I've gathered as I've been approaching my thirtieth birthday aren't so flattering. It's not such a big deal, and I normally don't make a fuss about it, but now I'm slightly petrified at the idea of being so exposed in front of Logan.

"Hey," he calls out. "The water good?"

"Frigid," I reply, just as a wave pushes me forward a bit.

Dreading the moment I'll be uncovered, I start to make my way out of the water. To avoid the waves that swell near the shore, I'm at least ten metres away from the edge of the water. It was one thing to get there, but it's quite another to get back out. The closer I walk to the shore, the bigger the waves are getting.

I spread my arms on both of my sides to balance myself, trying to focus on the way I'm moving my body instead of the fact I'm half-naked in front of Logan. I raise my eyes to see if he's looking at me.

Big mistake. The distraction takes my focus away from my proprioception and a wave hits me from a weird angle, pushing me straight into the water. I cough and flail my arms in surprise, and before I know it, Logan is knee-deep in the water, holding on to me.

He's got one hand on the small of my back and the other around my arm. My skin burns where he touches me. "Come on, here we go," he grunts as he helps me up and out of the water before the next wave has time to get us. Soon we're both away from the shore and standing on the dry pebbles, but I'm still coughing up seawater.

What a rookie mistake.

"You okay?" I've got both hands on my knees as I'm lurching forward, but I raise one hand to give him a thumbs up. Then I finally straighten up and see him looking at me.

His eyes travel from top to bottom, though I can see he's trying to do so in a subtle way. But it's not subtle at all. He stops for half a second on my middle, where my high-waisted bottom leaves a small strip of skin uncovered. I feel my face flush and immediately turn to pick up the towel I left on a nearby boulder.

His mouth is open in a soft O, and he finally blinks and looks away. I swallow the lump in my throat as I wrap myself in my towel to hide what shocked him so much.

Ugh. I hate when my anxieties get confirmed.

His footsteps against the pebbles ring out behind me. He's getting closer. "You sure you're good? Looks like you swallowed the whole ocean. And you look cold."

I don't turn to face him yet. Instead, I look out towards the ocean and take a deep breath. "I'm good. But, yeah, it's gonna take me a while to warm up, even with the sun being so strong."

I can move past this. I can ignore it. It's not like he'd be the first to not like what he sees. Jasper would consistently point out I was gaining weight and that I should be more careful.

So I plaster a smile on my face and turn to face Logan. "So yeah, I'm gonna go change."

He looks embarrassed, like he doesn't know what to do with his hands. So he crosses them in front of him, right below his hips. "Great, okay. And ..."

I don't speak, giving him time to continue.

"I know you've probably had enough water drama for

one day. But something came up and I thought you'd be interested?"

"What's up?"

He perks up. "The Zodiac place five minutes from the resort had a group cancellation. The owner, Yasser, always calls me when that happens in case people from the resort want a last-minute bargain ride."

I smile, liking the sound of that.

"So I thought we could take it for ourselves," he continues. "Hopefully riding around the water inspires something for your contract thing."

I want to say yes right away, but one doubt crawls in to stop me. "For ourselves? You know how to ride this thing?"

His eyebrows shoot up as if he's offended I've doubted his abilities. He puffs up his chest. "Of course. I've done it a few times when Yasser let me. It's pretty simple."

I cross my arms, careful not to disturb the towel. "Hmm. It does sound tempting." And that much was true. In fact, nothing sounded better than going out in the open waters for a little adventure. I've missed being on a boat.

Hey, maybe we'll even see a whale. If that doesn't give me some inspiration to inject some life into this website copy, I don't know what will.

But at the same time, I don't know if I feel like spending time alone with Logan right this second. I'm still feeling slightly hurt from the look he gave me. But it doesn't seem like he noticed, and really, it's not a big deal. Didn't I say I just wanted to be friends?

"It sounds tempting because it's pretty awesome," he

continues, raising his eyebrows even more. "So come on, what do you say?"

Whatever. I need to get over it. "Yes, let's do it."

—

After I get changed into some activity-appropriate clothing—some shorts and a tank top that dry quickly—I meet Logan at the lobby, where he's putting something in the trunk of his car. He stands back up and motions for me to get in the passenger seat.

"What do you have there?" I ask him as I point to the trunk.

"Just a few snacks in case we get hungry."

"Oh, now you're speaking my language."

Before I know it, we're on our way and already there. I think Logan exaggerated when he said this place was five minutes away. He probably meant five minutes on foot, because we've barely been on the road thirty seconds when he turns into the parking lot of a small, old-looking building. Beyond the building, I can see the docks lined with boats of all sorts: sailboats, fishing boats, and yes, a few Zodiacs, of course.

Excitement bubbles in my chest. Even though I've been to the ocean a few times, I've never actually been *on* the ocean. The closest I ever got was when Jasper and I took a vacation to Costa Rica and I begged him for us to go on the catamaran excursion, but it never happened. He'd preferred the four-wheeler excursion instead, and for some reason, he ended up winning the argument.

But this isn't the time to think about Jasper. I nearly jump out of the passenger seat of Logan's car and start sprinting towards the docks. "So which one is ours?" I yell out without even turning to look back at him.

"Wait up!" he yells back. "We need to sign some paperwork with Yasser first."

I turn back around to follow him inside the small building, where we sign our waivers. Logan assures me this is for legal reasons and that there's no actual danger.

Behind the counter stands a jolly-looking man with salt and pepper hair and a wrinkled face creased with laugh lines. He has a tidy mustache and warm, twinkling eyes. I assume this is Yasser. He pipes up to add:

"I've been running this business for thirty years, and we've only ever had two incidents!"

Instead of making me feel at ease, his comment adds a twinge of uncertainty to the whole thing. I hadn't really been feeling nervous before he'd said anything, but now …

I turn to Logan and cross my arms. "So you're sure you know how to operate this thing properly?"

"Of course. Come on." Now it's his turn to cross his arms. "Besides, it's really not that complicated. Any idiot can drive that thing."

"Not any idiot," Yasser interrupts. "Remember Ollie?"

"Oh, right."

I frown. "Who's Ollie? What happened to Ollie?" My breath starts to speed up. "Are you trying to make me nervous on purpose or what?"

Logan chuckles and places a hand on my shoulder. The

sensation immediately soothes me. I'm tempted to move in closer and lean my head against his chest, but I hold back. "You don't have to worry about it. Really, it's fine. We're gonna have fun." He drops his hand away and turns to face Yasser. "So we're good to go?"

"Yup!" Yasser hands a pair of keys to Logan. "She's all yours."

I'm no longer as giddy as I was before now that these two men have seeded some doubt about the safety of the whole thing. Still, I follow Logan outside and towards the docks. I stare out toward the sea. Beyond the wavy shore, the waters seem relatively calm. There's a flock of seagulls circling nearby, filling the air with their cries. It's a beautiful, sunny day. A perfect day for such an outing, actually.

This will be fun. Yup.

"Which one's ours?" I ask Logan as we make our way on the shaky docks.

"This one right here." He stops right in front of a large yellow Zodiac big enough for … I don't know, fifteen, twenty people?

My eyes go wide. "Are we going to be heavy enough to hold this thing down? It's huge!"

Logan laughs and hops on board to deposit the lunchbox of snacks he brought along. "It looks light because of the inflatable sides, but you don't have to worry. This thing's not going anywhere. Unless we get a tornado or a hurricane or something … which rarely happens." He steps back out and extends a hand. "You can go in first, and I'll untie it."

I take his hand, and a spark runs through me. I go still.

"You good?" he asks, his brows furrowed.

"Yup, yup," I reply as I nod, maybe a little too enthusiastically. I step over the side of the Zodiac, which is quite a feat for my short legs. Good thing Logan is holding my hand to give me a boost, otherwise, I would have probably fallen right into the water.

"You can get settled anywhere," Logan tells me as he starts to work on the knots. I look around the Zodiac—although it's roomy, there's not much seating space. I assume people would typically stand during most of the trip. But one large seat extends at the back, and two seats are next to the captain's spot. I make my way to one of those two seats, although the one in the back looks more comfortable.

Why? I ponder the question as I sit. *Did I sit here to be closer to Logan?* Obviously, and that's not good news. If I'm already too obsessed to sit far away from him, I don't have a chance. So I get back up and make my way to the seat in the back instead. I glance back at Logan. Luckily, he hasn't witnessed any of my awkward back and forth. He's still busy focusing on the knots.

It only takes him a few minutes to finish up and hop on the Zodiac. He's not that tall, but in comparison to me, his entry looks easy. Then I remember he has done this several times before.

Logan opens a metal chest near the side of the boat and brings out two lifejackets. He throws one my way. "Bundle up." We both put on our lifejackets, and Logan takes the captain's seat.

He shoots me a glance and a smile. "You ready?"

I nod, trying not to smile too hard. The previous anxiety I had about his skills is completely gone. Evaporated. The way he confidently smiles at me, the way his hazel eyes warmly twinkle in my direction, the way he looks like he was born to be here …

I want to melt.

Focus, Avery.

Logan starts up the motor, which starts rumbling below my seat. The vibration is soothing, almost meditative. And before I know it, we're driving away from the docks, speeding toward the blue waters of the North Atlantic.

The wind starts to pick up, and I notice my hair flying all over the place. I laugh and try to tame it with my hands, but it's useless. I give up and let it whip against my face. Logan glances back at me and grins, his focus returning to the waters ahead.

The scenery is breathtaking, with the sun shining down on us and the waves crashing against the side of the Zodiac. It feels like we are in our own little world, away from whatever is bothering me.

We're going faster now, speeding along with the wind in our faces. Logan looks over at me, a gleam in his eyes. "Hold on tight," he yells out.

I grip onto the side of the Zodiac, feeling the rush of adrenaline course through me. The water splashes up onto me. I feel utterly alive.

Logan expertly maneuvers the Zodiac, making sharp turns and sudden stops that send us flying. I scream with delight, feeling exhilarated by the sudden rush of speed and freedom. The wind whips my hair back in a frenzy, and I feel wild and reckless, like anything is possible.

We race along the coastline, weaving in and out of the rocky cliffs that jut out from the water like jagged teeth. As we get further out to sea, the waves grow larger, and the Zodiac begins to buck wildly in the choppy waters.

"This is awesome!" I yell to Logan, not even sure he'll be able to hear me through the wind.

But he does hear me. He turns back and gives me a toothy smile and a thumbs up.

I can't resist anymore. I want to be close to him. I want to tell him how exhilarating this is—how much this is what I needed. So I stand and make my way to the seat next to him, feeling the waves rocking beneath my feet.

As I sit down next to him, I can feel the electricity between us. Logan turns to look at me, and the intensity in his eyes makes my heart skip a beat.

He reaches out and gently tucks a stray strand of hair behind my ear, his fingers grazing my skin. I shiver at his touch.

"Are you having fun?" he asks, his voice barely audible over the sound of the wind and waves.

I nod, unable to find my voice. The rush of adrenaline coursing through me leaves me breathless and speechless.

Logan leans in closer to me, his lips almost brushing against my ear. "We can make it even more fun," he murmurs, his hand sliding down my arm and intertwining our fingers together.

Before I can respond, he expertly maneuvers the Zodiac,

and we shoot off towards the horizon again. The waves crash violently against the side of the boat, drenching us with salty water. But I don't care. I'm too caught up in the feeling of his hand in mine, the rush of the wind on my skin, and the sound of his laughter as we fly across the waves.

As I catch my breath, I glance over at Logan. He looks over at me with a grin, and I feel myself flush under his gaze.

That's when I notice how the waves have grown even larger, crashing against the Zodiac with a force that sends us flying. But Logan expertly navigates us through the stormy waters, his eyes never leaving the horizon. I can feel his strength and confidence radiating from him, and it's comforting to know that he's in control.

Only a few seconds later, I detect a shift in Logan's mood. His grip on my hand tightens, and he stares out at the water with a furrowed brow. Then he lets go of my hand, suddenly fully focused on steering this thing.

Seeing him not so sure of himself, I'm suddenly terrified. When did the sky get so dark?

The clouds overhead had been gathering for a while, but I hadn't paid much attention to them, too caught up in the rush of the waves and Logan's touch. Now, though, I can feel the hairs on the back of my neck standing up. The storm is coming, and we're out here in the middle of it.

I try to suppress the fear that's rising inside me, but it's no use. These waves are growing larger by the minute, and the wind is picking up speed. The Zodiac is starting to rock violently, and I can feel the panic rising inside me.

Logan's face is set in a grim expression, his jaw tight as

he tries to navigate us through the storm. Suddenly, a huge wave looms up in front of us, and I can feel my heart stop in my chest. We're going to capsize. This is it.

But just as quickly as the wave appears, Logan expertly steers the Zodiac towards it, riding the crest of the wave like a pro. I scream with both fear and exhilaration as we soar over the top of the wave, the wind and rain whipping against my face.

When I look up, I see Logan frantically trying to regain control of the Zodiac. Although his eyes show terror, he remains composed and collected. I don't know if he's doing it for my sake, or for his own, or if that's just how he is. Then he must see the look of terror on my face because he screams at me:

"You okay?"

"I'm fine!" I scream back. "Just focus on getting us back to shore!"

"On it!"

The next few minutes feel like hours as Logan navigates us through the storm, and the rain pours on us like the apocalypse is coming and there's no tomorrow. Unable to stop myself, I burrow myself into Logan's side and I hug his middle as tightly as I can. I have no idea how long I keep on holding him like this, but I pull away when I finally hear him curse loudly.

I look up at the same place he's looking, and I freeze as I see the huge wave coming our way.

Chapter 10

This is it. We're going to capsize. I'm going to drown.

For someone who loves water so much, isn't that fitting?

For a brief moment, frozen in time, I picture my mom. I see Sophie and her girls. And I even see my dad. But the last face to join them is Logan's.

I'm so stupid. I can't believe I'm this stupid.

I got the gift of a second chance with him. Something I never thought I would get again. It was a chance to explore what I truly felt—what I've always felt, deep down, even though I never faced it head-on.

And if this is truly my last moment, this means I've squandered that chance. And for what? To 'work on myself'? To take even longer than I've already taken to figure out why I can't just be happy?

I deserve this.

The wave crashes against the side of the boat, and suddenly I'm flying back. There's a thud against my back and a splash of freezing cold, and I realize we haven't capsized; the wave merely hit us.

Logan is next to me at the bottom of the boat, coughing up a storm. The splash from the wave must have hit him in the face. At least he's still got his glasses on his face.

"Logan!" I crawl to him and place a hand on his thigh, using it to pull myself onto my knees. He looks rattled but otherwise okay. I'm filled with relief, even though my body is shaking with the cold and the adrenaline.

When he finally manages to stop coughing, he looks straight at me. His eyes are big and wild. "It's okay."

"What if there's a bigger one? What if—"

His hand moves to cup the side of my face. "I'm here. This thing won't capsize. Trust me."

Time stops again. Suddenly there's no storm, no ocean, no wind around us. There's nothing but the two of us on this boat, and I'm not ruining this second chance.

Before I know it, I've leaned forward, and my lips are on his. There's a moment of hesitation—a single split second—before Logan's soft, warm mouth yields to mine. I gasp against him and part my lips for his tongue; I taste the salt of the ocean, but also something else that's undeniably *Logan*. Even though my body should be cold to the bone, I feel so hot that I think I'm going to dissolve in the rain.

With one hand still pressed against his thigh, I bring my other hand to wrap around his back and grab at his shoulder. His body moves with mine, and he wraps one arm around the small of my back to pull me closer. The contact burns at my skin, and I'm craving for more of *this*, more of *him*.

The hand that cupped my face slips into my hair as I lean into him. He lets out a low groan, which vibrates in my skull and lights me up like a thousand stars. The pressure of his chest against mine, of his hands pressing me closer, his mouth exploring mine … it's all frantic, urgent as if I'm about to slip between his fingers. I've sparked something within him I didn't know was there.

And I realize I'm not dissolving with the rain; rather, we're dissolving together into one entity.

There's a jolt from the side, which pulls me back to reality; another wave. I pull away from his mouth, even though my body is fighting to stay. "We need to get back," I rasp.

His eyes are hazy, his gaze intense. "Right." Like a robot that's just been voice-activated, he pulls away from our embrace and takes a seat back at the controls.

The wind and the rain are still going crazy around us, but they've already calmed down a lot more than before. The waves surrounding the Zodiac are nothing like they were just a few minutes ago. It's only a matter of time before this storm is over, but we can't take any chances. So Logan starts navigating us back into the fray, somehow knowing the way in the grey darkness.

—

We make our way back in a strange silence. There's a multi-faceted tension in the air, and I can't tell what it is I'm feeling. On the one hand, I'm still reeling from staring down the wave

I thought would be my undoing. And the storm, while calmer now, is still very present and looming around us. We're not safe yet.

On the other hand …

The feel of Logan's mouth on mine still lingers there. I don't know if my heart is hammering away because I was just scared shitless or because our lips finally met. The touch of hands in my hair and on the small of my back still lingers like a phantom.

Logan is fully focused on steering the Zodiac and getting us safely back to shore, which leaves me alone in my own head. The worst place to be.

Even though the moment has passed, I still feel frozen within it, like it's playing on repeat through my body and mind. And one thing is clearer than anything else—Logan kissed me back. There's no doubt about it. I'm not alone. What I've been feeling over the past few weeks isn't one-sided.

I don't know how to feel about that.

I'd promised myself I would hold back on these feelings for Logan. I'd promised I would figure my shit out first and not drag him in it. This is why I'm here. Yes, I'm writing copy for a fancy retreat website, but deep down, that's never what this was about. Because being completely uninspired for this website isn't the problem—it's a symptom.

A symptom of whatever disease has been crawling through my spirit like a parasite, leeching away my strength. My energy. My creativity. My courage.

It's no wonder Jasper left. Him leaving was never the reason I struggled to write this website in the first place. It was just a consequence—another symptom.

The night of our breakup, Jasper had said, "You know what? I'm done," his words dropping like a bomb as he crashed on the couch. He hadn't looked angry, or hurt, or sad. He'd just looked ... tired. Exhausted. "We're over."

"Wait," I'd cried out, standing in front of the couch like an idiot. The tears had burned the back of my throat like acid. "What do you mean we're over?"

He'd looked back at me, eyes full of ... pity. It had made me sick. It had made me realize he was serious. "I mean, I can't do this anymore."

"What are you talking about?" Part of me had wanted to get close to him, cup his face, and try to kiss it all away ... but I'd stayed frozen in the same stupid spot. "Where is this coming from?"

"I'm just ... forget it," he'd said with a deep sigh as he rubbed his face with his hand. "You can keep the place. I'll go to Italy like I was supposed to, then I'll figure out where to go. You don't need to worry about that."

"No, no, just wait a second." I could barely get the words out. "You can't just leave. This is coming out of nowhere. Come on—this is us."

"I'm sorry, Avery. I've made up my mind."

"No!" Panic had started to rise in my chest. "I need to know why! What did I do? Can you at least tell me what I did?"

His gaze had been stone-cold as he'd delivered the final blow:

"No, Avery, I'm done. I'm moving on. And so should

you."

He'd refused to give me an explanation. And I think I know why. He believed he was doing me a kindness by refusing to speak the real reason out loud.

You're not who you were. I loved you because you were a ray of sunshine. I would have killed just to make sure I could keep seeing that smile every day. And when that was the case, I could deal with the panic attacks. I could deal with your anxiety. They were like a package deal, two sides of the same coin. My little ray of sunshine who sometimes has a chaotic mind. But now? For months you've been going downhill. You barely go out. You're like a shell of a person now.

That was the truth we both knew, but he would never say it. Jasper always hated big confrontations, so he'd just refused to explain and left.

Like everyone always does.

Just like Dad.

I feel a pressure building up behind my eyes, a lump choking my throat. Despite having been with Jasper for so long, I'm not angry or upset anymore. I think I've accepted that he's gone. But my dad?

The man who always believed I could accomplish great things. Who would wipe my tears away when it was time for him to leave for another work trip. Who constantly promised he would always, *always* be there for me. That he loved me more than anything else in the entire world.

This man is now down south somewhere, gone from my life, from Mom's life. At first, when he decided not to come back from his next work trip, things were still normal between us. Of course I was devastated for my mom, but if he was no longer happy here, then I was happy for him to go chase that happiness elsewhere. Now that I'm an adult and no longer in school, he didn't need to be tied down to the family life that seemed to choke him.

But at least he talked to me. He responded to my calls. He checked up on me. Even flew me down there one February for my birthday.

Now I can barely tell whether he's alive or not. For all I know, his girlfriend could be holding him hostage in their basement and telling me everything is okay. Maybe the shame of leaving so suddenly finally caught up with him and he can't face me. Or maybe he wanted a fresh start with no daughter to tie him down.

Because even when he said he'd always be there for me, it was never true.

"I can see the docks!"

Logan's voice brings me out of my reverie. I look to where he's pointing, and he's right. The rain is clearing, and there, not too far away, the docks are coming into view. I'm not going to die at sea. What a relief.

Except relief isn't the only thing that washes through me when the Zodiac finally touches the dock. Fear is just as present, if not more. Because now that our lives aren't in imminent danger anymore, we won't be able to avoid the conversation for very long.

What does this kiss mean? I didn't stop to think about the implications on the boat. I know what I feel, but I can't help but think I'm taking a huge risk that just won't pay off. I'm only here for a short while, and so is Logan. Neither one of us is meant to stay. And what if he only kissed me back because of the adrenaline rush of being alive? Will I have enough time to figure it out if I pursue this?

I'm supposed to be here for work. To be alone. There's no way I have enough time to know what's happening between us before my stay is up. And even if Logan were to offer me a place to stay in the meantime, which is a *huge* jump—

Calm down, Avery—you just kissed, he didn't propose!

But even if he were to do that, he's leaving, too. And what happens next? I can't do this. Not again. Then I'll be right back where I began.

Without skipping a beat, Logan hops off the Zodiac and starts tying it back to the dock, single-minded to the task at hand. I don't move from the seat. Even though it's still raining and I'm freezing, I don't dare move until he tells me what to do.

From the corner of my eye, I see Yasser running straight towards us, looking crazed and shocked. I didn't know a man his age could run that fast. "Thank God you're safe! That storm came out of nowhere! I was so worried about you two." He kneels next to Logan, who's busy tying rope, and pulls the rope from his hand. "Give me that. Bring yourself and that sweet girl inside to get warm. I'll finish up." Logan nods at Yasser, looking a bit shell-shocked, and finally stands back up.

Now he's staring at me. He extends his hand to me, which I hesitate to grab at first. Who knows what that will do to me. But then I remember that I'm ridiculously short, and that going inside to hide from the rain will be the best thing to happen all season.

Maybe apart from that kiss. Or was that the worst thing? Ugh, I don't know.

I take Logan's hand, and our eyes lock for what seems like an eternity before he pulls me out of the boat. For once, I can't read his gaze. His thoughts are a mystery and it's eating me up. Does he regret what we did? Is he just still in shock? These questions bounce through my head as we run inside Yasser's shop.

Unsurprisingly, there's no one inside. Who in their right mind would come here during such a storm? I guess we did … but this storm wasn't on the radar. I'm about to stop walking, since we made it inside, but Logan, who hasn't let go of my hand yet, keeps pulling me forward. I follow without question as he leads us through a door marked 'Staff Only.' I'm assuming Yasser is okay with us coming back here since they know each other so well.

Inside is what appears to be a break room of sorts. The room is small but cozy, with a large window overlooking the stormy sea outside. There's a fridge and a couple of couches on one side, with a small table and a few chairs on the other. Only once we're right in the middle of this room does Logan stop and spin to face me.

I don't have a single second to say anything before he pulls me into an embrace. His arms are tight around my shoulders. Slowly, I wrap my own arms around him, burying my face in his soaked chest. I smell the ocean and sweat and something else that's undeniably Logan. The same scent I detected all those years ago when he held me in his room as

I cried my heart out the night Dad said he wouldn't make it to graduation.

"I'm so sorry," Logan blurts out, his voice cracking slightly. "This was my fault. I never should have ..."

My heart sinks. So he does regret it. He probably just kissed me back because I was the closest thing to him in a moment fuelled with panic. There could have been a complete stranger on board next to him, and he might have accepted a kiss from her, too. But it just happened to be me.

"No, no, it's okay," I interrupt. I pull away from his chest and am immediately stopped by the look in his eyes.

This isn't the look of a man who's sorry he just kissed the woman who was once his best friend. No—he is terrified. There's something completely wild about the lightning dancing in the hazel of his eyes.

"It is *not* okay," he interrupts back. Now he's holding the side of my arms tightly, as if I might still be taken by the wind. "I was cocky. I should have turned around as soon as I noticed the sky was getting dark. There I was, thinking that you can steer a Zodiac one or two times and suddenly become an expert in windy weather like this. I wanted so goddamn hard to make you have a great day, and instead, I put your life in danger like an idiot. I am so, so, sorry, Avery."

So he wasn't talking about the kiss. The fact that this could somehow have been his fault hadn't crossed my mind. Not even for one second. But I don't want to play 'sorry' ping-pong back and forth. Not right now.

Not until I figure out what the hell happened on that boat.

Because no matter how much I think it's a terrible idea, and no matter how much it terrifies me, I cannot deny, in that moment, as he's holding me closely, that I want it to happen again. And I want him to want it for real, not because of the moment.

"Logan." I stare straight into his terrified gaze. "I don't care. We're okay. We made it back. You got us back." I give him a soft smile. "You were pretty awesome out there, Captain."

Logan chuckles without humour. "But *I* care. God, Avery, if anything happened to you... I finally got you back, and now—"

"Logan," I interrupt him again. "I need to know. Did you mean it?"

"Mean what?"

"The kiss, Logan." I brace myself. "I meant it. Did you mean it when you kissed me back?"

He stares at me, and behind his eyes I can see his thoughts going a mile a minute. "How could I not?" he asks in an incredulous tone.

Before I can respond, his mouth is on mine.

Chapter 11

Logan's hands move to cup my face as our kiss deepens in a passionate, hungry way. Both of our bodies shake with all the longing we've kept hidden for far too long. Our bodies press against each other, desperate to be closer, as if trying to merge into one entity.

As our lips meet, my hands instinctively tangle in Logan's hair, pulling him closer, unwilling to let go. I can feel his heartbeat thundering against my chest, matching the rhythm of my own. Our tongues dance together in a heated exchange, exploring and teasing one another, lost in the moment.

Suddenly, I become aware of all the sensations on me: the rough texture of Logan's stubble against my skin, the rim of his glasses leaning against the bridge of my nose, the faint scent of saltwater still lingering in his hair, the warmth of his body enveloping me in a cocoon of comfort and desire. It's overwhelming, intoxicating, and terrifying all at once.

Is this really happening? Yes, it's happening. I can't stop it anymore.

As Logan's arms wrap around me, pulling me hard against him, I can't help but surrender to the feelings coursing through me. His fingers weave through my hair, gently at first, but his other hand soon finds my ass and squeezes. I moan against his mouth.

The sound of footsteps shatters our bubble, and his hands slip away as he pulls his mouth away from mine. I can still feel the ghost of Logan's touch as we step back from each other, our breaths coming in short gasps.

"Ahem," Yasser clears his throat, standing in the doorway with a raised eyebrow and amused smirk.

"Yasser, hey!" Logan says, his cheeks burning with embarrassment. "The boat's good?"

"It's fine," he replies, the corners of his mouth twitching with suppressed laughter. "I just wanted to check in on you two after all that … but I guess you're all good." His gaze doesn't linger long on me; it's clear he doesn't want to intrude any more than he already has.

Logan runs a hand through his tousled hair. Without even thinking about it, I do the same. "We'll live," he tells Yasser. That's when he turns to me, his face still flushed. But he's no longer embarrassed. There's concern etched into the lines of his face. "We should get you warmed up. You're shivering."

He's right about that. But I'm not just shivering because of the cold.

Yet, much as I'd like to throw myself back at him and shoo Yasser out of his own break room, I can't ignore the fact that my body is still chilled to the bone from the icy water. The North Atlantic is no Caribbean.

"Good idea," I murmur, suddenly feeling the weight of exhaustion bearing down on me. My limbs tremble, caught between desire and fatigue.

"Let's head to your cabin, then," Logan suggests, offering me his hand. "You need to get warm and dry. We can talk more later."

"Sounds like a plan," I agree, taking his hand and allowing him to lead me out of the break room. Yasser watches us go with a knowing smile but says nothing.

As we walk, I can't help but replay the last hour in my mind—the exhilaration of the open waters, the terror of the same sea once it unleashed its true self. And now that I know how Logan truly felt about the kiss, the memory fills me with warmth and longing for him.

It was a moment of desperation, but not just for any physical touch. It was a moment where his true desires came out along with mine.

Even though Logan blasts the heat as much as he can in his car, I'm shivering down to the bone. I want to talk, to acknowledge what happened, but I'm too cold to think. Or maybe it's the adrenaline finally coming down, leaving me defenseless.

Soon, Logan pulls up at my cabin. As soon as he's parked, I rush out from his car and fumble with my keys. Now I know exactly what I want.

I want him in my cabin, in my shower, with me. That'll warm us up.

"Come on in," I say as I open the door, my voice barely above a whisper. I walk inside and turn, leaving the door open.

Logan hesitates in the doorway, his hazel eyes searching mine for a moment before responding. "Avery, I—I don't think I should come in just yet."

Confusion clouds my thoughts as I process his words. Didn't he make it clear this is what he wanted? "Why not?"

"Look," he sighs, rubbing the back of his neck. "We've just been through something really intense, and … I don't want to take advantage." The way I want him right now, I can't possibly see how he would be taking advantage of me. "We're both still processing everything, and I want to make sure we're both on the same page before …" He weighs his words. "… anything else happens."

His honesty pulls at my heartstrings, making me appreciate him even more. But at the same time, the desire for him is so strong that it's hard to accept his reasoning. I bite my lip, trying to steady the whirlwind of emotions swirling inside me.

And I can't help but think this could be an excuse. Maybe, now that the adrenaline is out of his system, he doesn't really want this. Doesn't really want me.

"Just go get warm," he continues. "And then we can have dinner at the lodge later? I can pick you up after I've …" He gestures to his soaked clothes.

My heart thuds like a drum against my rib cage. Dinner. Okay. We'll have a chance to talk it out.

"Alright," I agree, trying to hide my disappointment. "Yeah. Good idea."

He smiles gently, his hand brushing against mine as he steps back. "I'll see you soon."

"Okay," I murmur, watching him walk away before closing the door behind him.

I make my way to the bathroom, peeling off my wet clothes as I step onto the cool tiled floor. Stream fills the room as I turn on the shower, enveloping me in a cloud of warmth. The hot water cascades over my body, soothing muscles I didn't even realize were tense. I tilt my head back, allowing the spray to wash away the remnants of fear and adrenaline that still cling to me like tendrils of seaweed.

As I stand beneath the pounding water, I can't help but think of Logan's hungry touch. The way it seemed like he couldn't get enough of me. My skin tingles at the thought made more intense by the cold thawing out of me.

I lather my hair and rinse it clean, the scent of lavender shampoo mingling with the steamy air. Smelling this scent feels strange. I haven't changed my shampoo in a long time, which means this is the same shampoo I use back home. The same shampoo I've been using all those years with Jasper. The scent brings back flashbacks of the two of us in the shower together—laughing, kissing, his weight pressing against my back. Oddly enough, the heartache that once overtook my entire being is only a whisper. Now all I want to do is chase this memory away and imagine Logan with me here instead.

When I've finished washing away the salt and the cold, I turn off the shower and wrap myself in a plush towel. As soon as I open the door, the steam disperses in the main room, and I see my bed.

I know I should get dressed right away. I'm not sure when Logan is coming back to walk me to the lodge for dinner. But the hot shower only made me more groggy than before.

Exhausted, I lie down on my bed, the soft mattress cradling my weary body. *It's only for a little while*, I tell myself, *just enough to regain my strength*. Just a little catnap.

As I lie there, the weight of the day presses down on me like a heavy blanket. The air in the room feels thick, saturated with the remnants of fear and adrenaline that still linger in my veins. Too tired to fight against the pull of sleep any longer, I let my eyes flutter shut.

—

I'm alone on a rowboat with nothing but ocean surrounding me in every direction. Above me, the night sky is clear, and I've never seen so many stars. The ocean is still, quiet, leaving room for contemplation of the stars above.

I feel … strangely at peace.

I remain seated in the rowboat for a moment, satisfied to simply take in this moment. Eyes shut. Deep breath in. Deep breath out.

"You've gotten pretty good at that." The voice startles me, and I open my eyes. I'm taken aback when I see Dad sitting right in front of me. But I knew it was him just from his voice. I'd recognize that voice anywhere.

"I had to." I cross my arms. "No thanks to you."

My dad gives me a sad smile. "I know. And you've turned out pretty good despite our little family curse."

"Pretty good?" I fight to keep my voice calm. "I think

that's a bit of an exaggeration. Don't you?"

He shrugs. "Do you?"

Anger starts rising through me. "Social workers. Psycho-educators. Therapists. I've gone through them all. And they all basically say the same things. Give the same tips. And it's not like you were around much to help me through it. That one time, maybe. Yeah, I've gotten better at knowing when the panic attacks are coming, and I know how to mitigate them, but … at what cost, really?" I take another deep breath. "I can't have a 'normal' job. If I weren't my own boss, I couldn't do this. I'm basically unemployable. I can't make friends. Going out where there are too many people is possible, but it's a struggle, and some days are worse than others. Plus, the man I thought I was going to have kids with left me. And the cherry on top? *You* left me. So, yeah, I think saying I'm 'doing good' is an exaggeration. I'm surviving, Dad. I'm not 'doing good'."

He doesn't say anything for a little while. Instead, he looks at me, his piercing green eyes staring straight into my soul. Then he finally speaks up. "Have you considered you're not supposed to be doing good right now, honey?"

"What do you mean by that? Didn't you just say you thought I was doing good?"

"Well, you are, given the circumstances." He looks out to the sea. "But I think you're looking at it from the wrong perspective, Avery."

This is getting annoying. "Are you just going to riddle me to death, or what?"

"You're trying to go back to who you were. Aren't you?"

"Maybe." Then I look back up at him. "But how do I go back?"

"You'll have to figure that out on your own … All I'm saying is, I think you're doing good, despite everything you're going through. I don't think I would have fared any better, my strong girl."

"But I'm not trying to be you," I argue. "So the fact that you wouldn't have done any better isn't some kind of milestone for me, Dad. I'm trying to be better. God, I love you, and don't take this the wrong way, but I'm not trying to model who you are."

"So, is that what you're afraid of?" he asks. "You're afraid of turning into me?"

"No!" I yell back, but I immediately soften. "Yes … maybe? Ugh." I let my face fall into my hands. "I don't know. I don't know anything. All I know is that I want a partner who's there for me, for our kids. And when I'm there, I want to be fully there. I want to go out and do things, even though the anxiety makes it so, *so* hard. I don't want to be the recluse who comes home after work, spends an hour or two in front of the TV, and then hides away in my room while the rest of my family moves on with their lives. I don't want to be that person, but I feel myself turning into that, day after day, because just existing is hard, and going out in the world is hard, and—"

"Shhh." I've begun crying, but he's holding me now. "It's okay, strong girl. I'm here."

"But you're not." It's just a dream.

"I know. I know. But he is."

"Logan?" I look up at him. "I can't rely on him like that. I can't live my life relying on someone else to function like a human being. I can't do that to him."

"Then don't." He strokes my hair, and oh, how I wish this was real. How I wish he was here. "Be a big girl. Work on yourself. But don't pass up a good thing, either. You can have both, can't you?"

"Can I?"

"I don't know, my strong girl. It's up to you."

Chapter 12

S hit, shit, shit.

By the time I've completely woken up, I realize how long I've been asleep. I don't know the time yet, but it's late enough for the sun to have set, which means it's at least 9 p.m.

Logan and I had agreed to meet for dinner. My heart sinks as I realize he must think I've ghosted him. Great. Just great. Just when I thought we were headed in the right direction.

I scramble to my feet and realize I'm still wrapped in my towel when it falls to the ground, leaving me naked. I roll my eyes and pick it back up to roll myself back in it just as the door cracks open.

In pops Logan's head. As soon as he makes eye contact with me, he recoils. "Sorry! I just wanted to check if you—"

I feel myself going hot all over. If he'd walked in just a few

seconds before, he would have seen everything. And while the idea makes me a little dizzy, I also find myself asking:

Would that have been such a bad thing?

"It's fine," I yell out so he can hear me from outside. I don't know if he's mortified or not, but right now that's not what I'm worried about. I'm overcome with guilt about having accidentally skipped out on dinner. "Logan, I fell asleep. I'm the one who's sorry. It was just supposed to be a little nap."

"I know." His voice is a bit muffled behind the door, even though he left a tiny crack open. "I came to check up on you earlier."

Relief floods through me—immediately followed by embarrassment. I was asleep—I don't know what he saw. Who knows how the towel moved around while I thrashed around the bed? Jasper always told me I moved like a hurricane in my sleep.

I think back to yesterday afternoon when Logan stared at me as I was coming out of the ocean in my bathing suit. Back then, I wasn't sure what he'd been thinking. His eyes had been difficult to read, but I had assumed he was shocked by my flabby middle.

But now that I've felt the intensity of his want when his lips were against mine ... I'm not so sure anymore.

But I know what I want. I want him to see all of me and like it.

I swallow, take a deep breath, and step towards the door. While one hand stays against my chest to keep the towel secure, the other opens the door.

Logan's reaction is immediate. His face goes tomato-red,

and he backs up just a little from the door, averting his eyes. "Um, hi," he stammers out.

His reaction confirms my theory. So it wasn't disgust after all. I curl my toes against my floor, trying to resist the urge to throw the towel away and jump into his arms. All in due time. For now, I'm still confused. "So why didn't you wake me, then?"

"You looked like you needed it." He pinches his lips and fiddles with his hands. It's cute to see him taken aback like this. And the fact he wanted to let me rest sends flutters in my chest. "Do you want to, um, get dressed, or …"

I chuckle. I need to put him out of his misery. Despite me knowing we both want this right now, I also want to take a step back and have a proper talk. This isn't some random guy I met on Tinder. It's Logan. I'm not about to ruin the friendship we've rekindled after seventeen years just for a bit of fucking.

Even though my body is telling me to do otherwise.

"Yeah, I'll go do that. You can come in. I'll go change in the bathroom." I turn and leave the door open, beckoning him inside. I can hear his slow, hesitant footsteps as he steps inside, but I don't look back for now. I walk to the foot of the bed, where my suitcase is lying open, and I grab something that hopefully won't be too distracting. A pair of emerald jogging pants and a matching sweatshirt should do it.

With my chosen outfit in hand, I make my way to the bathroom and shut the door behind me. Before I get dressed, I look in the mirror. Since I fell asleep with wet hair, it dried with a few weird kinks. I quickly brush through it and put on my clothes. There. I don't look like complete shit, but I don't look like a smoke show, either. This should be suitable for having an adult conversation about adult things without eliciting the hungry look I saw glinting in Logan's eyes.

When I walk out of the bathroom, Logan is sitting at the small table on one of the two stuffed chairs, staring out at the sea through the window. But his head immediately jolts when he hears me walk out.

I join him at the second chair. "So," I begin, leaning an elbow against the table.

"So." He doesn't move, and I can see from his expression that he's not sure what to say or how to behave.

"The boat."

"Yeah."

Ugh. This isn't going to be easy. I've never been the best at navigating these kinds of discussions, and from what I can tell, it isn't Logan's strong suit, either. But we need to get started somewhere.

I open my mouth to try again, but Logan beats me to it. "So here's the deal, Avery. I'm gonna be 100 percent upfront and honest, and I hope it's enough."

I shut my mouth and nod. "Go on," I whisper. My heart is trying to climb its way out of my throat.

"For a moment there on that boat, I got scared—really scared. And I'm not used to being scared like that. I pride myself on being pretty level-headed even in the most extreme circumstances, but this ..." He stares deep into my eyes. "This was different because you were there."

I stay silent, urging him to go on. It feels like time is

moving through molasses.

"Look, it's pretty obvious that I've always cared deeply for you. The day you left Red Lake was one of the worst days of my life. And the day you …" He trails off. My heart sinks—I know exactly what he's referring to. "Anyway. I moved on. I had my teenage life. I went to college, left for San Francisco, did all the things you're supposed to do. But I didn't forget about you, Avery. Not for one second."

I want to interrupt him, to tell him I never forgot about him, either, but I resist the urge. This is his time to speak.

"And how could I? We were so close. I never got close to anyone like that, ever again, you know that?"

A hint of sadness sweeps through me. We were only thirteen when I left. He can't be telling me that, in all that time, he's never gotten close to anyone?

At the same time, I already believe him and know what he means. I love Sophie to death, and she gets me … about ninety-nine percent of the way. Even if we've been friends for ages—for much longer than Logan and I were ever friends—I don't think we'll ever get that last percent.

And I don't think everyone gets that, ever. I'm sure some people go their whole lives without finding someone who truly, deeply *gets* them like Logan once did for me. Like he could again.

Even Jasper, whom I really did love, and whom I believe loved me back for a time … I can't even say he 'got' me as much as Sophie did. Maybe ninety-five percent.

So while it makes me sad that Logan never got close to anyone like he did with me, I see how that's possible. He's cute, whip-smart, caring … but even I remember the protective shell he wore around his heart at all times. The tough exterior most could never crack. Even when he was being bullied, I was the one who reacted more strongly than he did. Nothing ever got to him, or at least, he never let anyone see that it did. No one except me.

"When you arrived here, the last thing I wanted was to dump all of that on you. You came here stressed out, tired, and fresh out of another relationship. And even though I never forgot about you, it had still been seventeen years. So I held my tongue.

"But on the boat, Avery—in that split moment where I thought there was even the slightest chance I could lose you—and when you kissed me … All of that fell away. I couldn't live with myself—or die, for that matter—without returning the feelings you were showing me. So that's how I feel."

I relive the moment and feel my toes tingle. During that moment, I made Logan's shell crack. And knowing that it's possible to make that shell dissipate, even for just a second, excites me to my core.

"So, yeah, I meant it. I don't think I've ever meant anything more than I did at that moment. I can't explain how it felt to have you kiss me like this. And now that you've felt what I felt, I don't want to lie to myself and say I want to pretend it never happened, because that's not what I want."

Now I have to speak up. I have to hear him say it. I have to be sure. If there's even a single doubt, I won't do this to him. I won't impose my broken self on this person I love so much. "Tell me what you want, Logan."

Our eyes don't waver from each other. "I want you back in my life. I want what I've been secretly hoping was possible for the last seventeen years. I want what I thought I could never have. But I don't know if that's what you want. Because most of all, I want you to have everything *you* want."

The words come stumbling out of my mouth before I can hold them back:

"I want you."

We both sit completely still, staring at each other as if frozen in time. I'm the first to move when I lean over the table, pausing right before we meet.

He's so close now that I can feel his breath on my lips— shivers go down my spine. I close my eyes and take a deep breath to steady myself right before I lean in the rest of the way.

He tenses up slightly right as I press my lips gently against his. Underneath the reaction is the unbelievable softness of his mouth. I'd barely had any time to register the sensation before, but now, I'm fully here in the moment, as if frozen in that singular moment of impact.

His hesitation gives way to helpless yielding as he moans against my mouth. His hands find my waist and pull me over the table and right against him, right on top of his thigh so I'm straddling him as he stays seated. I follow his movement and wrap my arms around his neck, letting my tongue slip into his mouth.

My mind is racing while my entire body goes online. The sound of my own heartbeat going a thousand kilometres an hour echoes in my ears while I feel the roughness of his stubble against my cheek. The warmth of his cheek, the taste of his tongue—I'm drunk with all of him.

His fingers trail up and down my back and send shivers along my entire body; I moan softly into his mouth and press my chest up against him with urgency. The thigh pressing between me is driving me insane, building up the pressure within me.

"Logan," I gasp, and he smiles into my mouth.

"God, Avery," he speaks in return. "You're so soft."

I slip a hand underneath his shirt and feel the warmth of his skin beneath my fingertips. He groans into the kiss, and his hands finally find their way to my ass, gripping it tight.

I feel high on something new. Even though I've wanted him for a long time, I never pictured him as someone with a sexual hunger. It makes no sense. Of course, I knew he had one. But feeling myself in the line of sight of his hunger is almost more than I can take.

He begins to pull at the hem of my sweatshirt, and I resist the urge to ask him to go faster. I can't rush this. I've waited much too long to rush anything, almost my entire life. I can wait a little longer and savour everything this moment can be. So instead, I place my hands on his and help him slide the shirt off as slowly as I can.

Since I didn't put on a bra when I got dressed earlier, he's met face-to-face with my bare chest. I watch as he takes in a sharp breath. His eyes drift to my breasts, then slowly make their way back up to meet mine.

"You're perfect," he whispers, taking in all of what he sees. The desire in his gaze overwhelms me with love and sends a rush of adrenaline pumping through me. I can hardly breathe just looking at him like this.

But I can see him hesitate. I arch my back, offering him a better vantage point—and simultaneously increasing the pressure against his thigh. That seems to have done it; he trails his hands up to my chest, teasing me, not quite touching me where I want him to.

"Fuck, Logan," I gasp when his thumb strokes my nipple. I throw my head back and gasp again. I've never felt a need this strong, lightning this strong, just from this type of stroking.

"Avery," he groans, his voice thick with desire. I pull my head back and meet his mouth again, but soon Logan is pulling away from my lips and trailing his way to my neck.

I know exactly where he's going and the anticipation is killing me. I weave my hand through the waves of his hair, almost holding my breath.

I almost cry out when his tongue finds my nipple. My head falls back again as he continues to tease me with his mouth, softly and tantalizing at first, but then more firmly. The world around me fades away into nothing but Logan's warm breath on my skin and the gentle tug of his lips and tongue.

This is so right. How could I not see it before?

Pressure is mounting within me, and I shift against him, pressing my chest more firmly against his mouth. But even though I love what he's doing to me, I need to feel his mouth on mine again. Gently but firmly, I guide his face with my hands until our lips meet.

That's when I feel him starting to unbutton his shirt now

that his hands are free. I can't wait to touch what's underneath, to feel more of him under my fingertips.

Keeping our mouths together, I slide one hand underneath while he's still working on his buttons; I trace the outline of his abdomen, tight and hard. The last time I saw his chest, when we were kids, it was completely smooth. Now I feel hair under my fingers, with smooth, taunt muscles underneath. There's an irresistible heat that radiates off of him.

My hand works its way up his chest while the other helps pull the shirt off entirely. I break from the kiss, only to take one look at him. He isn't big and bulky, but lean and strong. Exactly how I like it.

"Is this okay?" he whispers in a hoarse voice.

"More than okay," I sigh. "Please, touch more of me, Logan."

Now that his hands are free, they come back to cup my ass; they slide underneath my cotton jogging pants and find the soft flesh beneath. His touch makes me pulsate at my core. My toes find the ground only to lift myself up from his thigh so he's able to slide the pants down.

I'm about to sit back down on his thigh, but he stands from the chair before I have the chance. Next thing I know, he's right in front of me, the hair on his chest tickling my breasts, and I'm fighting against the belt buckle at his jeans. Beneath my hands, I can feel the swell of him—how much he wants me.

The pressure is so intense that I can feel tears welling up in my eyes. Our mouths meet again, hungry, a mess of tongues and teeth and lips, until I've finally loosened his belt and pulled the jeans down.

He pauses, his hands still hovering below the fabric of my underwear. His eyes look deep into mine. "Are you sure?" he asks, his voice deep and husky.

God, I'm going to pass out.

"Yes," I whisper back, and that's enough to have him grab me by the waist and push me backwards. Suddenly, I bump into the bed behind me, and Logan pushes me into it, crushing me with his weight and his mouth.

There's nothing between us anymore, nothing except a strong hand that glides from my hip to between my thighs. He slides his fingers underneath the front of the fabric that's there, and I gasp as I feel his touch. Logan's touch. My back arches to urge his hand to touch more of me, but he's painfully slow, teasing me, so gentle and soft with his movements.

I run my fingers through his tousled hair as he works his magic, while I try to move one hand towards his boxers. But he stops me with his other hand. "Not yet," he grunts against my teeth. "I've waited so long to touch you like this, Avery. To return the favour." The memory of that night is vivid but so far away at the same time. "I need to ..." His hand stops, and his lips begin to make a trail of kisses down towards my breasts again. But this time, he keeps going, down past my breasts and toward my belly button.

I hold my breath in anticipation. I know what he's going to do, and I already feel like I'm going to break apart just at the touch of his tongue.

His hot breath teases the sensitive skin, making my hips jerk up involuntarily. I gasp as his tongue flicks against my navel, trailing lower still until he's at the edge of my underwear. He looks up at me, his eyes now dark with lust. "Can I?"

"Yes, please, yes," I urge him. His fingers slide under the lace again, then pull down to pull the underwear away. The world narrows to just his touch, his breath on my skin, the anticipation building within me.

He wraps his arms around my thighs and slowly pulls them further apart just before I feel the tickle of his breath against me. I sigh, then moan as he begins, gently at first but then with more fervour.

"Logan," I gasp, unable to think of anything else but this man, this perfect man, this gentle and loving man who holds me at his mercy. And for the first time in forever, I can't think of anything but him, and us, and the two of us together—not a single drop of anxiety can reach me in this moment.

My hips push up against my will, and I can't breathe, I can't breathe, I can't breathe—

Until I come undone, wave by wave, and hear myself scream Logan's name.

Soon, he's looking up at me, slowly working his way back up to my mouth. I feel the bulge of him against me, and I'm swollen with more want.

It seems like climaxing didn't relieve the pressure; instead, it keeps building, and against my will, I'm clawing against his boxers as his lips find my ear.

"I'm going to lose my mind seeing you like this," he says hoarsely. "You're everything I imagined and more. You're so beautiful, Avery."

"Logan, please," I beg him, my voice just as hoarse as his. My entire body is trembling beneath his. "I want you. All of you." My hands finally manage to slide his boxers down, and I wrap my hand around him—he jerks and inhales sharply.

But then his demeanour changes. He backs away, and my body cries out, suddenly cold and alone without the weight of him. "Shit," he says. "Do you have condoms here?"

I look at him, confused, and my heart drops. No. I'm not letting this ruin the moment.

That's when I remember what he told me earlier. "Are you …" I don't know how to say this without breaking the mood. "Because you said earlier … five years?"

He looks confused for a moment, but then it registers. "Oh. Um, yeah. I've been checked. I'm clean. But …"

"Me too," I whisper back. "And I'm on birth control." I look at him, practically begging him with my eyes. God, he's so beautiful, standing over me like this. "Logan, please."

I can see he's resisting, but my begging takes him over the edge. The hunger comes back in his eyes, taking over whatever else was fighting against this urge. He comes back against me, covering my entire body. "Are you sure?"

"I've never been so sure of anything in my life." It was always meant to be like this—just the two of us. I can't imagine anything more right than this. I wrap my hands around his lower back and pull him closer. "I need you inside me, Logan. Please."

A groan escapes his lips, and we kiss again, slowly this time, as I help guide him with one hand. His first thrust is slow, deep, and has me crying out against his mouth.

He pulls back immediately. "Are you okay?"

"Yes," I whisper, hardly able to speak. "Yes. Yes."

"Fuck, Avery," he groans as he pushes back inside me. I can't help but gasp at the feeling of being one with him as our bodies move together with the backdrop of the ocean's rhythm outside. At first, we're slow, deep, loving, and I hear him whisper my name against my mouth. But it doesn't take long before we both lose ourselves in the motion, the sensations, the deep ache, and before I know it, I'm begging him again. It's enough to send him over the edge, and I fall along with him, lights going off in my vision, unable to remember anything but his name and the feeling of his body with mine.

Chapter 13

The first thing I'm aware of when I awaken is a pang of hunger.

Oh, right. I haven't had dinner.

But that's immediately followed by the sensation of Logan's bare chest against my back, his arm wrapped around me, and his breathing against my neck. I'm reminded of another time, from so long ago.

But this time, it's different. This time, it feels right, and there's no shame in my heart.

My heart is already dancing in my chest, and I've been awake for all of five seconds. Feeling Logan's taut, naked body against mine like this fills me with a joy that's hard to comprehend. I'm completely, utterly satisfied. I'm exactly where I need to be.

I close my eyes and let myself be completely consumed by this moment. Outside, I can already hear the waves

awakening. There's a small ray of sun making its way through my curtains, landing just a few centimetres from my face on the bed.

I wish I could bottle up this moment forever. Because I know that outside of this little bubble of peace lie archers, ready to shoot and pierce through it all.

His steady breathing suddenly changes. He takes one long inhale and exhale, stirs, and immediately squeezes me more tightly against him. He's awake. "Good morning," I whisper.

"Good morning." His voice is still hoarse, but he's smiling through his words. He leans over to kiss me, softly at first, but then with more intensity as it awakens our hunger once more.

Shortly after, we're both panting and breathing heavily. Part of me wants to stay in this bed forever ... but the other part of me is absolutely starving. Not for Logan—for actual food. And I'm craving my morning coffee. But just as I'm about to tell him I'm making breakfast, Logan pulls away from me and gets on his feet.

"You're probably starving, right?" He walks to the other side of the bed near the chair where most of his clothes lie. I can't stop staring at his lean body, the taut muscles, the slight V above his hips. "I'm gonna head to the lodge and grab us some breakfast. You stay right here."

"You're the best person in the entire universe. You know that, right?" I sigh while he's getting dressed. I stay in bed, wrapped up in the cushy comforter, watching him lazily, hungrily.

He looks at me and smirks. "See, that's where you've got it all wrong. Because that person just so happens to be you."

"Bah," I reply with a chuckle. "I'm not gonna have this argument on an empty stomach."

"Exactly. I'll be back soon." Now fully dressed, he approaches the bed and kisses me again, this time breaking away before it can turn into something more. "Stay."

While he's gone, I obey him and stay put. But with him gone, the anxious thoughts are starting to crawl back into my brain.

What are you doing?

He's going to leave when he figures out just how much of a mess you are.

You're not moving here, and who says he's going to move to Montreal with you?

What about what you did?

He deserves better.

Each thought is like a hot pin through my skull. There are happy ones in there to switch things up, but soon they're overwhelmed by the others.

Deep breath in.

Deep breath out.

My phone starts ringing, and I jump. For a moment, I have no idea where it could be, then I remember I'd put it in the pockets of my jogging pants, which are on the floor. I scurry to the ground and search for it until I see who's calling.

It's Sophie.

I answer immediately. "Hey!" The sound comes out of my mouth a bit strangled.

"Hey, how have you been?" her voice chimes on the other end of the line. In the background, I hear Gwen singing what sounds like *Baby Shark*.

I hesitate for a second, not sure what to answer. Because I don't even know. How have I been? And do I tell her about what just happened?

"You okay?" When she asks that, I realize I've been silent for too long.

"I had sex with Logan," I blurt out before I can stop myself. I hear a gasp on the other end of the line. "Twice. He's out to get us *breakfast*, Soph."

"Good for you!" Sophie cheers. "If that doesn't inspire you, I don't know what will."

"I don't know what to feel," I sigh.

"Happy. You should feel happy."

"It's not that simple."

"Actually, it is that simple." Before I can reply, Sophie continues: "You know you're allowed to be over Jasper, right?"

"It's not that." I rub my eyes and sigh. "I didn't even think about Jasper."

"Good."

"I just … Sophie, I don't know what I'm doing!"

"Relax. It's okay. I'm here for you, remember?" Her voice is gentle, but there's her usual edge, reminding me that she's not going to take any of my bullshit.

"So what do I do?"

"You know what?" She sighs. "I'm coming down there before you screw up what could be a really amazing thing for yourself."

"What? But what about—"

"The baby? I can handle the baby, Avery. Honestly, I

could use some time away from Gwen." She whispers that last sentence. "She loves being a big sister, but sometimes it's a bit much."

"But—"

"No buts. It's decided. I'll take the next flight to Sydney and rent a car there. Executive decision. Love you. You can tell me all about it then." And before I can argue any further, she hangs up.

I stand there, completely naked with my phone against my ear, when the door opens, revealing Logan with two coffees and a bag of something that smells nice. "I could get used to walking into this kind of scene," he says, his voice getting husky. As he closes the door, his brow furrows. "You okay?"

"I ..." I lower the phone from my ear and stare at it, still shell-shocked. "I guess you're going to meet my friend Sophie?"

"She's coming here?"

"Apparently." I take a deep breath, then shake my head to bring myself back to the moment. "But more on that later. Right now I'm mostly interested in what's in that bag."

I quickly get dressed while Logan takes the food out of the bag to place everything on the table. He brought back a chocolate croissant, two breakfast sandwiches, a chocolate chip muffin, and a few apples in addition to the two cups of coffee.

What did I do to deserve this man?

I nearly throw myself towards the table once I'm fully dressed. Without waiting for permission or politeness, I grab the chocolate croissant and scarf it down, taking gulps of coffee in between. Logan just eats one of the breakfast sandwiches and watches me swallow my meal, slightly amused.

I barely talk during breakfast and end up eating the remaining breakfast sandwiches, the muffin, and one of the apples before I'm satisfied. Afterwards, I open the curtains and sip on my coffee. I take a moment to breathe before I allow myself to think about everything that just happened in the last twenty-four hours.

Outside, I can see the ocean and its waves crashing against the rocky beach like it does every day. I channel the sound of the waves to calm my nerves and gather the courage I need for what comes next.

"So, what is this?" I finally manage to say. Logan bites into the last apple and stops mid-bite. When he hums in confusion, I quickly gesture between the two of us. "This. Us. What is this? And what's next?" Asking the question makes the end of my fingertips go numb with anxiety. I love what's happening between us, even if it scares the shit out of me. But I have too many questions.

For one … How serious was Logan when he made his confession last night?

I want you back in my life. I want what I've been secretly hoping was possible for the last seventeen years. I want what I thought I could never have. But I don't know if that's what you want.

It sounded pretty clear when he said it, but he didn't explicitly say he wanted me in the same way I want him. Because I don't just want what we had last night. I, too, want Logan back in my life—and not just as a friend.

I want to wake up next to him every morning. I want to share everything with him. I can already imagine what it would be like to work side by side—him programming, me writing for a client.

But I can't tell him that—not yet. That's going to freak him out. So I need to know what he's expecting, what he really wants. Because right now, we don't even live in the same place.

Logan swallows his bite of apple and gives me a teasing smile. "I guess we're going to have to figure that out, huh," he says in a teasing tone.

"I know this probably isn't your idea of sexy post-coital pillow talk," I start, "but I just … you know me. I don't deal super well with uncertainties." He nods, waiting for me to continue. "For instance, what's next for you after your summer working here is done? Headed back to San Francisco?"

Suddenly, his carefree smile is gone. He's got a slight frown. So I guess he's worried about the future, too. We've really opened up a can of worms by doing what we did last night. And again this morning. "It's okay if you are," I start, hoping I'm not giving him the wrong impression. "I'm open to discussing … you know. What that would look like. I just need to know we're on the same page."

"Yeah, it makes sense. We'll figure it out," he says, almost ending the sentence like a question. He turns his gaze to look outside. He's clearly got his mind on something.

"Well … yeah. That's what I'm trying to do." I try not to sound annoyed, but I think it goes through anyway. "So … Are you going back there in the fall or not?"

"I don't know," he sighs. He's still not looking at me.

"What do you mean you don't know?" His response weighs on my chest. I have no idea where this worry is coming from. Minutes ago, he was carefree, looking as happy as can be. There was so much love in his eyes that I thought I was going to overdose on it.

What's going through his mind?

Maybe he regrets what we did. I feel a pit in my stomach. He never explicitly told me what he wanted. Maybe I got it all wrong.

"I mean, I don't know yet," he replies, exasperated. He closes his eyes and takes a deep breath. "Sorry. I'm just a bit tired. Didn't get much sleep last night." He looks at my chest and shoots me a playful smile. He's back. "Got distracted by a few things."

"Oh. Okay." I'm a bit relieved his good mood is back. He's just tired. That's probably all it was. "So, you're actually considering working elsewhere? Are they going to let you work from home or something?"

Logan looks at his phone. "Actually, Avery," he starts as he gets up from his chair, "can we continue this conversation another time? As much as I'd love to laze around all day and go back to bed with you …" He leans to kiss me. I savour as much of it as I can before he pulls away. "I need to go to work. I promise we can continue this soon, okay?"

"Oh. Right." For a moment, I'd forgotten he works here. And I'd forgotten I came here to work, too.

"But we should have dinner. For real, this time." He winks at me. "If I come here and find you napping again, you can be sure I'll wake you up." To clarify exactly what he means, he bends to kiss me again, slowly and passionately. One hand weaves in my hair while the other holds my shoulder; I wrap my arms around his back and pull him closer.

The kiss ends too soon. He pulls away with a smile. "Okay. Gotta go for real. I'll meet you back here at six?"

"Okay." I watch him leave, still feeling the warmth of his lips on mine.

Once he's gone, I quickly change into shorts and a T-shirt—my official 'work uniform' when the heat starts rising in the morning. I then take a five-minute breather outside to integrate the ocean air as I sip my coffee, then go back inside and get settled for what I hope will be a more productive day.

The first thing I notice when I open my email inbox is an unread email from Leslie. I click on it, silently dreading the reply:

Avery,

Ok—we are DEFINITELY getting somewhere. I like the new version you sent us SO much better.

Please proceed with the rest of the website pages using this approach. The rest of the team would like to see a draft ASAP.

Best,

Leslie

Relief washes through me. I'm finally getting somewhere. I don't know if it's because of the time I've been spending with Logan, or the ocean air that's finally filled my bloodstream, or just a matter of perseverance, but I'm starting to think I can actually finish this project without getting asked for a refund—which I would be unable to provide, in either case.

With an extra boost of motivation from this feedback, I settle down and write. It's a bit difficult at first; from time to time I start wondering exactly when Sophie will end up here. That, or I'll think back to the way Logan dodged my questions. But eventually, I'm able to reach the elusive flow state from which I create my best work.

Something I haven't been able to do for a long, long time.

Before I know it, it's already 5:30 p.m. and I'm rushing to get ready before Logan arrives. Now I'm much more nervous than the first time we went for dinner. Last time, we went as old friends. Now, we're going as … what, exactly? I don't know, but I do know one thing:

This is very obviously going to be a date.

Maybe the last time had even been a date.

Ugh, I don't know.

I look at my reflection in the tiny bathroom, not sure what to do with myself. My hair dried weird from falling asleep on it wet yesterday, and I don't have any more time left for a shower. Instead of trying to tame the weird kinks, I brush through them and tie my hair back into a messy-but-cute bun. Then I pull out a few strands to frame my face. Not too bad.

Next, I get changed into a yellow floral dress that's supposed to be a mini dress but reaches a bit below the knees on me. A few final flicks of mascara, and I'm ready.

I look at myself one last time, satisfied. For the first time in a long time, I feel like I can call myself beautiful. I guess seeing a man succumb to your charms twice in less than twelve hours will do that to you.

I've got a few minutes left, so I take out my phone and start texting Dad.

I'm sure you would have called it Dad, but I think Logan and I are a thing? I haven't felt this happy in ages. Even when I was with Jasper. This is different. I can actually be with myself around him and he never says any offhand comments. He doesn't mind the family curse. It's like he was created to counter it, you know? To soothe my anxiety.

I hit send and let out a deep breath. At this point, I'm not expecting anything back. But I still feel like I have to try.

I hear knocking, and my heart skips a beat. Only then do I realize how much I've been holding back on the feeling of missing Logan for the entire day. I nearly run to the door.

On the other side is Logan, wearing a black short-sleeved button-down shirt that makes his sun-tanned skin pop. In one hand, he's holding a bouquet of flowers. They're lilies.

"I was hoping they're still your favourite," he says, handing the bouquet over to me. I close my eyes and take a deep breath, inhaling their sweet aroma. It's going to be okay.

"They are," I confirm with a smile. "They're beautiful, Logan. Thank you." From his demeanour, it seems like the weird mood he was in this morning is gone. I'm hoping it was just a fluke.

After I place my flowers in a vase inside, we make our way back to the lodge by foot to find Logan's car. He's taking me back to The Coastal Kitchen, but this time he says we're going to take advantage of their patio. Apparently, we can spot the ocean from there. I don't know how I didn't realize they had a patio the first time we came, because I'll choose a patio over any indoor seating when I can.

We have a drink, then two. I order the shrimp pesto pasta again because I decide I love myself and want to enjoy nice things. Once again, he's greeted by the staff and some regulars, but this time when a middle-aged man remarks about bringing his girlfriend, his reply is different:

"This is Avery," he says, beaming right at me.

Not 'Oh, she's just a friend,' not 'Oh, no, it isn't like that,'—he just lets the girlfriend comment slide right past us without discomfort or awkwardness.

And when he inevitably gets asked to play the piano, he looks at me and asks if that's okay. Of course I want to hear him play. The last time I heard him play was the moment I realized how I felt about him.

But something else goes through me at that moment. A moment of boldness. I have no idea what I'm thinking when I say out loud:

"I should sing!"

Unfortunately, I'm not a singer. Well, okay—my voice is cute, and I can sing in tune, so I'm not a complete racket. But I'm far from pop star material, and I've always known that. Despite all that, I just love singing my head off. And tonight, something makes me want to live fully and express myself.

It makes no sense that the last time I was here, I struggled to make it out without panicking, what with all the people coming to talk to us.

But it is what it is. I'll take what I get.

Logan looks at me with surprise, which soon transforms into glee. "Okay, let's do it."

Once we make our way inside, the restaurant is buzzing with chatter and the typical sounds of people eating. But as we get closer to the piano, Logan pulling me by the hand, the restaurant suddenly goes quiet. I can feel the weight of everyone's gazes. They know Logan. They don't know me. Who am I to bust into their world like this? I'm about to change my mind and turn back, but Logan is already at the piano, looking at me with a twinkle in his eyes. This is exciting to him.

I can't turn back now. I don't know what this moment means, but it means … something. I've got to commit.

"What do you have in mind?" Logan asks in a low enough voice that the diners can't hear him. That has to be pretty low—we could almost hear a pin drop. Even the wait staff is talking more quietly, their eyes turned toward me with inquisitiveness.

"What about *My Heart Will Go On*?" Logan makes a face, and I burst into laughter. "I'm kidding, I'm kidding. As if I could pull that off."

Logan, looking relieved, chuckles with good nature. "Okay, what about … just follow my lead." He braces himself to play, and in a moment, the restaurant is engulfed with the musical notes of *Stand by Me*.

Great. That's an easy one for my range. I can do this. My heart is about to bust out of my chest, but I can do this.

I take a deep breath and begin to sing. At first, my voice is shaky, and my fingers start going numb, but I place a hand on the piano to steady myself and look at Logan who's already looking back at me. He's not even looking down at the piano keys; he only has eyes for me.

That seems to be enough to keep me steady. His eyes say everything. That I can trust him. That he can trust me. That we can stand by each other, and the rest will be fine. Like the first time I heard him play, I'm overtaken by a magical sense of awe surrounding the entire room.

The last notes of the piano decay, and there's a moment of silence before the restaurant erupts into applause. For a moment, I can't move. Next thing I know, Logan is standing next to me, sweeping me into a romantic embrace.

His lips touch mine in a way that seems to say:

She's with me, and I'm proud of that. This is for the whole world to see.

I kiss him back with all the appropriate ardour of a restaurant. I have to focus all of my will on holding back from making a fool of myself. When Logan pulls back, I'm slightly dizzy.

His hand softly strokes my jawline. "You have a beautiful voice," he tells me. "Everything about you is beautiful."

My face goes hot. I look away, feeling embarrassed, yet so happy to be seen like this. Logan has always looked at me like no one else does. Like he fully sees every part of me, for better or worse. Like even my deepest, darkest flaws have a way of seeming beautiful from where he's standing.

It's a shame it has taken me this long to realize why he looks at me this way.

I'm so shaken that Logan has to guide me back to the patio so we can finish our meal. And I'm so high up on my cloud that even the curious gazes of the diners don't bring me down.

Outside, the sun is setting. Despite this, the air is still warm. Perfect, in fact. We both sit back at our table just in time for our meals to arrive. It's like the universe has given the word to line everything up perfectly at the same time.

I don't take a bite just yet. Instead, I reach out to touch Logan's hand. His hazel eyes stare deep into mine, stirring something loose inside of me.

"Logan," I begin, my voice hardly more than a whisper. "I—"

A ringtone erupts and stops me mid-sentence. I'm taken aback and pulled out of this perfect bubble, this dream. The sound is coming from Logan. Confused, he fishes his phone out of his pocket and takes a look at the screen. That's when his face goes dark.

My stomach sinks. There's a new pressure on my chest. I've been here for nearly two weeks, and I've never seen an expression like this on his face. In an instant, I dig in the back of my mind for memories of young Logan. But there's nothing there. Nothing that resembles this.

Something is deeply wrong.

"I have to take this," he says flatly right as he stands. He doesn't make eye contact with me. "I'm sorry. I'll be right back."

And he leaves me alone at our table, my unspoken *I love you* dying on my lips.

Chapter 14

The wind ruffles through my hair, bringing the scent of saltwater with it. The boulder is hard against my back, but I can't bring myself to care enough to switch positions.

I'm staring out at the ocean, watching each wave lap the pebbles at my feet. The sun is bright against my eyes; I should have put on sunscreen before heading here. But I wasn't really thinking. All I knew was that I needed out of my cabin.

There's no use trying to get into flow today. I could already tell from the moment I placed my fingers on the keyboard. It didn't stop me from trying for a good two hours, but here I am regardless.

After Logan came back to the table, his mood had very clearly shifted. He was no longer wearing the dark look from before, but gone was the excitement, the lightness, the care. He just seemed … tired. And I didn't dare ask him what the

phone call had been about. I couldn't bring myself to, even though I wanted to know more than anything else at that moment.

So we finished our meals without much else to say. At least, I finished my meal. Logan hardly touched his. Then he drove me back to my cabin, saying he'd be calling it a night. He felt queasy, he'd said.

Of course, this being Logan, he was apologetic and sweet about it. And he didn't leave before kissing me goodnight and leaving me wanting for more. Still, I can't stop thinking about the way his entire face changed when he saw who was on the other end of that phone call.

A million scenarios swim through my mind. An ex-girlfriend come to haunt me. His doctor letting him know he has cancer. A loan shark calling in his debt under threat of breaking both his legs and killing his new girlfriend while at it.

This is stupid. The ex-girlfriend is the most plausible, but even then, Logan has given me nothing to make me believe I should be worried. And unless he lied to me, he did say he hasn't really gotten close to anybody, so even that scenario isn't so likely. Whatever it is, he's not ready to talk about it.

But the possibilities weigh on my chest. After all, if it was just something silly, couldn't he have let it go to voicemail while we enjoyed our date? No—whatever it was, it was serious enough to interrupt the perfect moment we'd been having.

Unless he didn't perceive that moment the same way I did. After all, if he truly cares about me as much as I care about him, wouldn't he want to tell me about whatever is going on? Wouldn't he want to confide in me and ask for my support? Wouldn't he want me to stand by him as he deals with whatever is on the other end of that line?

I know I would. If I received a devastating phone call, the first thing I would want to do is cry on his shoulder.

It's dizzying to realize how deep these feelings for Logan go. Even now as I'm staring out at the sea, my entire body aches for him.

I'm pulled from the innards of my thoughts by a voice that's calling my name. I stand and turn towards the short cliff where my cabin stands, and there she is—Sophie. Tall and elegant, waving at me from afar with baby Heather strapped to her chest.

Warmth and relief flood through me at the sight of her. I run back towards the cliff, already silently thanking her for making the trek all the way to Cape Breton just to speak to her crazy best friend, because what I need more than anything right now is a friend. And not one who'll sweep me off my feet and make me cry out their name in the dark.

"Holy shit!" she screams at me as I'm making my way up the wooden stairs that lead up the cliff. "This place is sick! Just look at this view!"

"I know, right?" I'm about to hug her, but with Heather in the baby holder, I'm not too sure how to proceed. Sophie laughs and pulls me in a hug anyway, careful not to squeeze Heather too tightly in between us.

"This better be inspiring for you," she laughs in my ear. "Otherwise, I'd say you're pretty much doomed." We break apart, and Sophie takes a good look at me. "Okay, don't take this the wrong way, but you certainly don't look inspired."

"I've had a weird day," I explain. And a weird night. I kept waking up after the same nightmare, over and over again. It was of Logan drowning after falling from that stupid Zodiac. Every time, there was nothing I could do but watch helplessly as the waves overtook him.

So, no, I don't look my best this morning. I don't own the type of makeup Sophie has, the type that would hide these dark shadows under my eyes. I also haven't taken the time to change from my flannel shorts and stained T-shirt I used as pyjamas.

Sophie, on the other hand, is positively radiant. You can hardly tell she's been wrangling an infant or just got off a last-minute flight. Picture a supermom in your mind, and that's Sophie. "I met your guy, by the way," she tells me as we're walking back to my cabin.

My insides clench. I hadn't even thought about my two best friends meeting. And without me there? I hope it wasn't a disaster. "Oh," I simply say, afraid to ask how it was.

But of course, Sophie goes on. "He's super cute. And also not too tall for you." Sophie is, in fact, taller than Logan. Not that I mind. "I can definitely see the appeal. So how was it?"

I flush at the memory of the two of us entangled in my bed. But it's immediately overshadowed by last night. How weird he acted. And how I'm still not sure what to think of it. "It made me realize how much Jasper and I were actually kind of incompatible," I explain. Even though the words are there, my tone is off, and I know Sophie will sniff me out.

"But?"

"But he's being really weird, Soph."

"Weird how?"

I recount the events at dinner last night as we both sit at the picnic table just outside my cabin. Sophie nods along as she takes her daughter out of the baby carrier and starts breastfeeding her.

"Okay, yeah, I can see why this would make you worried," Sophie starts, "but honestly, Avery? It could be a myriad of things. And even if he cares a ton about you, you can't assume he'll want to spill his guts on all the shit that might be going on in his life right now. He's a guy. You know how closed-off guys can be."

I grunt in response.

"Take Matthew, for instance." Sophie pauses to adjust Heather's position at her chest, then sighs. Did I just see her roll her eyes? "If I didn't constantly ask, I would never know what's bothering him. Like, I know we've had a baby not so long ago, but if I hadn't asked him what was up, I don't know if we would have slept together since I gave birth."

"So what was up?"

Sophie opens her mouth, then smirks at me. "Oh, no you don't. This isn't about me. I'll rant about Matthew later." Now it's my turn to roll my eyes at her. "Anyway, if I were you, I wouldn't worry about it. Whatever Logan's going through right now, it probably has nothing to do with you." She suddenly jerks her head to look at me intently. "Oh, by the way, I invited him out to lunch, just the three of us!"

My eyes go wide. "You did what?"

"Well, how else do you expect me to get to know him and decide if I approve of him?"

Deep down, I know she's probably right. Sophie and Logan getting to know each other is the logical next step, especially if Logan truly is serious about something happening between us. But the two separate sides of my life colliding like this feels strange.

There's too much out of my control.

As we head back to my cabin, Sophie lets me know we're meeting at the lodge at noon to eat out on the patio. To kill time before then, both Sophie and Heather take a short nap while I shower.

When noon rolls around, I'm looking a bit more presentable. I changed into a clean pair of non-PJ shorts and a light blouse, and even though I couldn't completely get rid of the dark circles, the shower did help revitalize me a bit. This is the best I'll be able to do.

We head to the lodge's patio together. Sophie and I get seated, and she leaves Heather in her baby carrier next to the table. She's content to play with a crinkly toy next to her mother. It doesn't take very long for Logan to come out of the lodge and find us.

As soon as he does, our eyes meet, and he doesn't seem to notice how much of a mess I am. I don't know exactly what he sees, but it makes his eyes mellow out and become alive. In fact, his entire posture changes. Seeing him like this is a soothing balm over whatever wound I've been tending to.

For that brief moment, I forget about last night, and I just want to rush into his arms. But I exercise some restraint, to be polite. At least, I think that's what I'm supposed to do with Sophie here.

I scratch my throat and gesture to Logan. "Sophie, Logan, I believe you've already met?" My voice comes out high-pitched.

Logan looks at Sophie for a brief second. "Nice to see you again," he says politely, right before leaning in to kiss me. The world stops moving, and Sophie's no longer there—but too soon, the moment ends, and the kiss is over.

"So," Sophie says as she crosses her arms on the table. She's got a huge grin on her face. "You're going to have to fill in a few gaps for me, Logan. Avery's been my best friend since she arrived in Montreal, but I've hardly ever been able to pull anything out of her from the before times."

The next hour is perfectly pleasant; Sophie and Logan get along well and each trade embarrassing stories about me from their respective time with me. I notice Sophie stays away from any stories featuring Jasper, which I'm thankful for.

At some point, Logan asks about our high school graduation prom, and I tense up. Sophie dives straight in: "Oh, yeah, you know what? I was never able to figure that one out. Avery didn't even come. She went to graduation, received all her awards—that *nerd*—and then she skipped the prom afterwards. And I never got a straight answer on that one. Maybe you know something I don't?" Sophie's tone is playful, so I know she's only trying to keep things light and fun. But Logan frowns, and I know he knows why I didn't go.

He shoots me a questioning look. He doesn't know how much I want him to say. I sigh and give him a slight nod.

Sophie is looking inquisitively at me, then at Logan.

"I'm going to go out on a limb here and say that's got to have something to do with our grade seven graduation party," Logan explains. There's a new sadness in his eyes, mixed with something more. I don't know what he's remembering, exactly. My face gets warm and my insides clench.

"Grade seven grad party?" Sophie asks, clearly puzzled.

"Remember how I arrived in Secondary Two?" I remind her. "Well, in Ontario, grade school stops at grade eight, and high school starts at grade nine. So I would have missed my grade school graduation."

"Oh." A look of understanding crosses her face. "So you had a grade seven party instead?"

"We tried," Logan begins. He can see how painful it is for me to retell. How embarrassing. So he hesitates, unsure if I want him to continue.

"But as you know, Sophie," I say with a sigh, "I'm not so good at making friends."

The table falls silent for a moment. The air is heavy. Years later, it still cuts deep to remember how no one else showed up for me. It ended up being just Logan, me, and both our moms in Logan's backyard. So, I didn't want to be reminded of this when high school came to an end.

That's why I didn't go.

Sophie was my only real friend, but she had other friends apart from me, and they all had boyfriends while I'd just been dumped—which seems like a recurring theme for me. I didn't want to feel like the odd one out.

"From the moment I met her when she first arrived, we

were inseparable," Logan explains, his voice soft. "But I guess no one else saw what I saw."

"It's a shame," Sophie begins. "I never did understand because I find her to be absolutely awesome." She gives me a big grin and places a hand on mine. "And anyone who can't see it is either stupid or not worth our time. Or both. So I'm glad you've been able to see it, Logan."

—

After lunch, Logan goes back to work, and Sophie and I head to the beach. I take her to a real sandy beach, Ingonish Beach, after which this town takes its name. While I love the beauty of the pebbly beach below the resort, I've been craving a sandy beach for a while, and I know Sophie loves them, too. Plus, it's much easier to set down a baby in the sand.

Because Sophie seemingly plans for everything, she even brings a small pop-up beach tent specifically designed to keep babies in the shade. It's a perfect day to be here; it's hot but not too hot, the sun is out but not too scorching, and the waves aren't as intense as other days. Other people are here, too, but not to the point where I feel claustrophobic or where we have to fight for a small spot of sandy estate.

Sophie lays her daughter down in the tent; Heather happily squeals and moves her little arms and legs with glee. Right as Sophie's done tending to the infant, she turns to me with fiery intensity in her eyes. "So, you've got nothing to worry about," she states as if she's never been more certain of anything in her life.

"What do you mean?"

"That man is in love with you."

I'm stunned, speechless. My fingertips feel numb. How would she even know such a thing? She's known Logan for hardly more than a few minutes.

Sophie rolls her eyes. "I know that face. And believe me, I'm right. That man looks at you like you're the eighth wonder of the world. Which, for the record, he's not entirely wrong about." She winks. "He's sweet, he's cute, and you're letting your anxiety ruin a perfectly good thing if you don't allow yourself to see that."

"But how can you be sure? Love is a big word," I argue. The doubt and dread are snaking through my veins like ice. "It's pretty obvious he cares about me, but to go so far as to say he's in love with me? And before you say it, I can't *ask* him that! It's mental. We've only been back in each other's lives for, what, two weeks? Hardly that. So I can't know for sure."

"No, you can't," Sophie confirms in a dry tone. "But we can't ever be sure of anything, ever. Except for one thing: I'm certain you're going to be miserable if you come back from this trip alone. How long are you going to keep feeling sorry for yourself until you actually do something about it?"

"That's the thing," I say. My throat constricts as tears start to gather behind my eyes. "Maybe you're right, but maybe you're not, and it's not that I'm feeling sorry for myself … it's that I'm not sure if I'm …"

Maybe I'm too broken and messed up for this to work.

"Honey." Sophie grabs me by the shoulders and looks squarely into my eyes. Her gaze is intense. "Honestly. I know you think you're kind of fucked up or whatever … but believe me. We all are. At least to some degree. You think I don't cry myself to sleep in exhaustion some nights? Well, I do. You think I don't want to murder Matthew some days when he's annoying the hell out of me or leaving his dirty socks all over the place? Of course I do.

"But that doesn't stop me from showing up and doing what I do best. Being a mom. Running my business. Being an absolutely amazing partner to Matthew. I can do all of that, and I still have parts of me that I'm ashamed of sometimes."

I pause for a moment, taking all of that in. She's got a point, I know. But she doesn't know everything. She knows about my dad, and about the way I've been feeling for months, and about my anxiety. But she doesn't know what I did to Logan. How I hurt him. And how this shame makes me doubt I truly deserve him, even if he truly is in love with me.

"We didn't tell you the whole story about our grade seven grad party earlier," I begin, feeling my chest tighten. I've never told this story out loud before. Well, I've never told it to anyone, period.

Sophie raises an eyebrow. "Go on."

I take a deep breath, feeling my hands quiver. "After nobody came, we watched a movie with our moms, and then I stayed over at Logan's place. Just before we went to bed, I downed my first drink. A rum and coke."

Sophie makes a face. "Way to get started there, champ. You couldn't start with a beer like normal teens?"

I ignore her comment and keep going, my stomach clenching. "Usually, I'd sleep in a cot in his room, but this was going to be the last time I'd sleep over at his place. We were packing the next day and moving right after that, so I asked him if I could sleep in his bed."

This time, Sophie doesn't make an attempt at a witty comment.

"This being Logan, of course, he said yes. And I fell asleep on his chest. The sound of his heart beating against my ear lulled me to sleep." I take another deep breath. "I woke up in the middle of the night, and somehow we were spooning. He had his arm around me, but I don't think he noticed. He was fast asleep. We probably ended up there by accident, without even meaning it. It's like it was the most natural thing in the world for us to end up like that. And by then, I was still feeling a bit … uninhibited from that rum going through my tiny thirteen-year-old body."

This is so stupid. Why am I struggling to tell this part? It's not even that big of a deal. After all, Logan and I had sex just yesterday morning. This old piece of our history shouldn't matter. Why should it?

Yet, somehow, it does. I'm nearly trembling by now.

"I felt him against my back. And … God, I don't know, Sophie—I really don't know what came over me. I'd never even kissed a boy by then. I think I was feeling turned on, but I'd never felt like that before. I was confused at the way it made my body feel. So I just let my body do what it wanted to do."

"Wait … did you …" Sophie looks at me with big eyes.

"No, no, we didn't have sex," I explain. "We just fooled around a bit. And we kissed. My first kiss. His, too." My ears are red-hot.

"Avery," Sophie's voice is no longer in her tough-love tone. She's softer, quieter. "I'm pretty sure what you just described is perfectly normal. At thirteen, your hormones will get to you. Plus, you drank, and you shared a bed … I mean, I wouldn't have expected anything less from two horny teens."

"I just—" The tears are coming out now. "I felt so ashamed afterward. I wasn't sure he was happy with what we did. I kind of just … went at it. What if he wasn't ready? What if he didn't see me that way?"

"There's nothing to be ashamed of," Sophie reminds me. She scoots closer and wraps an arm around my shoulders. "Plus, now you know he does see you that way."

"I'm no longer ashamed of that part," I sob. "I'm ashamed of what I did because of that shame I felt back then. That's what I did wrong."

Chapter 15

Sophie's staring at me, waiting for me to go on. And I'm trembling.

"When I got to Montreal and started school with you, I developed a little routine," I start. My heart is pounding, and my ears are ringing. "I'd go home, head to my room, grab my laptop my parents got me as a consolation prize for moving, and head straight to MSN."

"Oh my God. MSN. That was another era, wasn't it?" Sophie chuckles.

I try to chuckle along to lighten my mood. It doesn't really work. "Yeah, it really was. So, I'd wait for Logan to log on too. And for the first two weeks, we didn't miss a single day. We'd chat, send each other funny cat videos on YouTube, all that stuff. You and I weren't quite friends just yet, so that really made the transition easier."

"Yeah, I remember," she interjects. "You were kind of

weird at first. A bit closed off. I didn't want to scare you off by being too forward." She chuckles again.

"This was nothing like hanging out in real life, and I missed him so much," I continue. There's a weight on my chest, and it's starting to burn. "But it was better than nothing at all. Despite that, we didn't speak a single word about that last night at his house. I didn't dare to bring it up, and neither did he. And every time I'd even think about it, I'd feel gross. My heart would sink." Back then, I didn't understand what the hell had come over me that night. It was like someone else, another Avery entirely, had taken over my body and started hungering over Logan like I'd never done before. And thinking about the incident did weird things to my body— more things I didn't understand.

"And that was the issue, or at least part of it, because we didn't talk about it, I had no idea how he felt about it. He didn't seem upset about it, but it was hard to say. You can never tell when you're texting. And so every evening during those two weeks, I'd wait with anticipation until he logged on … but I felt more and more anxious about it every day." I pause to take a deep breath.

"Are you okay?" Sophie checks in.

I place a hand on my chest and shut my eyes. "I will be." I need to finish my story. I open my eyes again. "I felt this huge unspoken thing between us, and the weight of it was suffocating me. Plus, there were those other feelings. I think—" I look out towards the waves. "Back then, everything was so new. The anxiety was new, the move was new … so I couldn't decipher all that stuff from each other. But I think

…" I turn my head to look back at Sophie and swallow. "I think it was love."

There. I've said it. Sophie's eyes go wide, but she doesn't say anything yet. The truth is, I can now look back at myself all those years ago and understand what I was going through. And I recognize these feelings I'm feeling now.

I love Logan.

And not for the first time.

My eyes start to burn. "And back then, I just wished so hard that I could go back to how it was before. I wished I could see him in person and just hold him and ask him what he thought. How he felt about everything. So chatting with him on MSN was both my favourite and least favourite thing in the world … all at once.

"And one day, he logged on and started chatting. But I just found myself staring at the message. Unable to move. It was like I was frozen in place and watching myself from outside my body." The light trembling in my body has evolved to full-on tremors, and the tears start falling down my cheeks. "The minutes ticked by, and Logan kept asking if I was there and waiting for a reply, but I couldn't. I had a panic attack right then and there."

I don't tell Sophie that this was also the first time my dad walked in on one of my panic attacks. I don't tell her about the way he held me against his chest and stroked my hair more gently than he'd ever done. How, after I'd calmed down, he told me it wasn't my fault but rather his. How I'd inherited the panic attacks—our family curse—from him. How he promised he would do his best to teach me how to get through them.

My dad kept his word, at least, for the most part. He showed me a few breathing techniques and taught me the basics of meditation. But it didn't completely fix it. Nothing really does. You can manage anxiety and panic attacks, but you can't cure them. And Dad wasn't there as often as he said he'd be.

"And I felt so ashamed, Sophie." My voice is shaking, but Sophie tries to steady me by touching me lightly on the shoulder. "I know now that I shouldn't be ashamed of my panic attacks, but back then, it was so new. I felt so broken. And every time I wanted to start chatting with Logan …" My voice trails off.

"You had another panic attack," Sophie finishes for me. Her voice is softer than ever. She stays quiet, waiting for me to continue what I have to say.

But my silence confirms it. She nailed it right on the head.

"Did you ever …" Her question is unspoken, but we both know what she means to ask.

"No. I never spoke to him again." The words hurt coming out. I shut my eyes as if trying to keep the shame out like I'd keep the sun out. But I don't try to keep the tears from falling.

Deep breath in, deep breath out.

"At some point, he convinced his mom to call our house number, despite the long-distance fees. Mom picked up and looked so happy to tell me it was Logan on the other end. But that sent me into an immediate panic. Mom said I'd call him back later. I never did. He gave up after that."

We're both silent for a while, letting the story hang in

the air. I can almost feel the pain I inflicted on Logan back then in my own body now; it prickles my skin like a thousand needles.

It wasn't fair. I was so selfish not to try more. And by the time I'd gotten a better grasp on how to somewhat control these panic attacks, it was too late. Too much time had passed. I couldn't bring myself to call or send him another message after all those years.

How could I? How could I open up that wound again? I just assumed he'd moved on, made new friends, and forgotten all about me.

But I never forgot about him. When I made my Instagram account, I checked almost every week if he was on there. It took years for him to pop up. From time to time, I checked up on him to see what he was up to.

Because I love him.

And evidently, he must have done the same; otherwise, how would he have known my favourite song? Does this mean he feels the same way I feel?

"Avery." Sophie gives my shoulder a soft squeeze. "I think you did the best you could under your circumstances. I can't pretend to know what it's like to have anxiety or panic attacks … I really can't. And for that, I'm thankful every day." She sighs. "And sure, from Logan's perspective, it must have really, really sucked." Those words jab in my chest. God, how I wish I could have acted differently. "But he knew about your panic attacks, right? Didn't you tell me he used to help you through them?"

"Yeah." My voice breaks into a sob. "He knew."

"Then there's a good chance he figured out what was happening when he called and when your mom saw you panic. He can't have known the whole story or understood why you were reacting that way, but I'm sure he knew you didn't stop talking to him just for the heck of it, or because you no longer cared about him."

"Maybe." There isn't much conviction in my voice.

"And even with all that, Avery …" She squeezes my shoulder again. "He's obviously over it. I saw the way he looks at you. That isn't the face of some guy who's still upset over whatever happened seventeen years ago. So if he's over it, when are you going to give yourself permission to get past it, too? When are you going to give yourself permission to just be happy for a change? Christ, Avery." She looks straight at me. "You're an amazing person—I don't say that lightly—and yet you're so hard on yourself all the time. You know you don't have to self-flagellate all the time, right? You know you're allowed to just be happy without having to deserve it?"

Her words echo in my brain; I mull them over as I watch the waves lap the sand.

Chapter 16

Sophie doesn't stay in Ingonish Beach for very long. She and Heather sleep in my cabin for the night, and the next day, she's already gone. But I'm okay. I'm going to be okay. I had her for long enough, I think.

Her words mull around in my brain for a while, even after she's left. And I figure that she has to be at least partially right. After all, my anxiety does seem to make everything worse, so I don't know if I should trust it. Of course, it's going to tell me I need to worry about everything and that things won't work out between Logan and me. Of course it will.

That's what it does.

But I have permission to not listen to it. Because Sophie is right; I deserve to be happy. Apart from a few weird incidents, Logan has shown me that he cares. And every time I'm with him, I feel surrounded by a warm halo of light, and the inspiration that makes me feel alive stirs back up within me.

The dull darkness that has been holding me back for so many months now is nothing but a pale shadow when he's around.

So I've got a chance to be myself again. To be happy again. I'm not going to let anxiety ruin it for me.

Not anymore.

After Sophie leaves, Logan and I fall into a comfortable routine. I wake up every morning with him next to me, which is enough to fuel me with all the inspiration I need to get my work done. But before he leaves, I can never resist pulling him close, and we end up tangling together and unable to let go, even if we've already done so the night before. He can't get enough of me; I can't get enough of him.

It's intoxicating.

At some point every morning, he does have to let me go and head to work at the lodge. I spend my days alternating between writing, walking along the rocky beach, dipping in the cold ocean to wake myself up, and grabbing lunch at the lodge when it's time for Logan's break. Once or twice he comes to surprise me with a hot lunch and a coffee while I'm still writing, and it sets my entire body ablaze.

When evening falls, we either go out for dinner or he'll make me something in his apartment above the lodge. We always end up on our bench facing the ocean, and we talk. We talk like the world's ending tomorrow and we'll never get another chance to speak. We talk to catch up on seventeen years of not talking at all.

The days are exactly how I'd pictured them when I booked this place. The inspiration is flowing like a magical river through my fingers. I'm getting much better feedback on the quality of the website copy, and it's somehow meeting their near-impossible expectations. I'll be finished before the month is up, which will give me more time to think about what I want next for Logan and me.

And the evenings are exactly what I need. Having someone to listen, someone who can truly see me as I am, makes it easier to keep everything else under control. And it certainly doesn't hurt that when we close out the evening in my bed, Logan knows exactly how to please me. Every caress, every kiss, every wave of us coming together is yet another piece of proof that tells me this is exactly right. Our bodies fit together perfectly, just like our minds. And finding him again, coming together like this again ... it's almost worth the seventeen years we've had to endure apart.

That's what I'm thinking now as we pull up to the parking lot in the middle of the woods. The day is a bit overcast but still quite hot, so I'm glad Logan's 'special spot' is in the relative coolness of the forest.

"So this is where you wanted to take me after our first outing?" I ask as I exit his car. I take a look around and whistle. "Yup, definitely a great murder spot. I can just picture it at night."

Logan erupts into laughter; the rumbling laugh I just can't get enough of. I look at him and once again try to take in the reality that he's mine.

It seems too good to be true.

Not today, Avery. Anxiety is not going to win today.

I push the nagging thought aside and laugh along with him. "You weren't supposed to remember that part," he says.

"Now I'll never get away with it." Once he settles his laughter down, he grabs a small backpack from the trunk of the car. We've got a few essentials stocked in there: water, a handful of granola bars, sunscreen, and bug spray.

Once Logan is ready to go, he points toward an opening in the woods. "It's this way." I begin to walk towards the opening, my steps eager.

As we walk, I look around and can't help but admire the beauty of the trail. The forest is mossy with several huge boulders and fallen trees, and the trail in front of us meanders along a small stream. The scent of the moss and running water is both refreshing and exhilarating.

We walk in silence for a few minutes while Logan lets me admire the surroundings. But when I finally turn my head to meet his gaze, he's staring at me, his hazel eyes warm and caring.

"It's beautiful," I whisper, taken aback by the way he's looking at me.

He doesn't break the stare. "It really is." My heart skips a beat, and I suddenly want nothing more than to stop this hike and jump into his arms, press my lips against his, and hear him moan my name.

But instead, I simply grab his hand and keep going.

The rest of the path is pretty easy, even if I'm a bit out of shape. Logan doesn't tell me what's at the end of the path, but about halfway there I begin to hear the faraway sound of waterfalls.

I stop dead in my tracks, overtaken by giddy joy. "Where are we headed, exactly?" I can't help but ask, my voice coming out way higher in pitch than I intended.

Logan gives me a smug look. "We're almost there. You'll see."

I can't help but pick up the pace; my limbs are wound up from the excitement. "Oh, now I know it's gotta be a waterfall," I squeal. Even though I'm walking faster, I still tread carefully. Now that we're deeper into the woods, roots stick out of the ground, twisting around fallen tree trunks all around us.

The closer I get, the louder the falls echo in my ears. The smell of water against stone—petrichor—blended with the mossy woods is intoxicating. I quickly glance behind me to make sure Logan is keeping up with me, but I've got nothing to worry about; he's right at my heels, that huge grin of his plastered on his face.

When I turn back, I finally begin to see the falls across the bendy trees. I break into a run but quickly stop in my tracks when I see the shallow pool at my feet. Wasting no time, I remove my shoes and my socks to dip my toes in the pool at the bottom of the falls.

It's pure bliss.

The water is cool against my hot skin, and towering over me are the falls cascading over mossy stones. Tall trees surround the area, making it feel intimate and hidden away. There's no one else here but Logan and me, so nothing stops me from giggling with glee as I splash my toes in the water.

"You know why I like this place?" Logan asks, removing his shoes to join me in the shallow pool. "I mean, apart from the obvious?"

I look at him, and I can't stop smiling. My cheeks are starting to get sore. I think I know what he's going to say. "It's very similar to the hidden falls we found with my dad at Kakabeka Falls, isn't it?"

There's a glint in his eyes, and I know I've hit the nail on the head. The main falls at Kakabeka were stunning, but the three of us ventured into a lesser-known trail while my mom rested at our campsite. And even though the hidden falls we found were much smaller, we all felt connected in that moment.

I blush as I recall what my dad had said to Logan to tease him. "Remember how my dad encouraged you to put your arms around my shoulder for our photo in front of the falls?"

He rolls his eyes. "Yeah, I remember. And I also remember how he told me to never touch you again after he'd taken the photo." I laugh, and he laughs with me. It was all said in good fun.

God, I miss Dad. A sharp pain blooms in my chest.

But it's quickly forgotten when Logan moves his hands to my hips. "I've been coming here two, three times a week. At least before you showed up. Because it would bring me right back to that moment with you. And for those brief moments, I could pretend you'd never left."

My stomach drops. He doesn't add that he could pretend I'd never ghosted him, but I know he's thinking it. My chest tightens, but I blink a few times and sigh as I keep my eyes closed.

I lean against his chest; one of his hands travels to my lower back. Inhaling his scent along with the smell of the falls, I'm overwhelmed by how safe I feel with him like this.

There was a time you felt safe with Jasper, too.

And with Dad.

I wave the thought away; what would Sophie say? She'd tell me to stop overthinking. So I try to do exactly that.

I look up at him with expectant eyes. His pupils dilate, and he seemingly understands the look I'm giving him because both his hands shift down to grab my ass. The contact lights up a fire in my lower belly; I press myself even closer to him and wrap my arms around his neck, bringing our lips together.

Here, alone in the wilderness, the kiss is slow and tender, unrushed. I part my lips and welcome his tongue as I weave my fingers through the hair behind his neck. Logan softly runs his thumb from behind me to the underside of my shirt, tracing a line all the way to the underside of my bra. I gasp into his mouth when his hand presses underneath the fabric of the bra to cup my breast, and my hips jerk. When I feel the hardness of him pressing against my belly, the pressure between my thighs cranks up a notch—or two.

Logan pinches my nipple between his thumb and index, and this time I moan. "You make me feel so good," I gasp against his mouth.

"God, I love touching you, Avery," he grunts in response; his hand runs over my stomach, inching lower and lower until it reaches the top of my leggings. "I want to make you feel good."

A flash of hesitation goes through me. There's no one else here, but anyone could easily walk in on us like this. The anxiety wants to reign it in, but another part of me finds this extremely hot.

Logan's hand pauses. "Unless you don't want to?"

"Yes, Logan, please," I urge him, pushing his head with my hand so our mouths connect again. But his hand moves painfully slowly, circling just around my waistband in a teasing motion. I push myself up on my tiptoes to urge his hands closer, to relieve the pressure that's aching there.

Ever so slowly, Logan slips beneath the stretchy fabric. I whimper as his fingers stroke gently, just around where I want him to go. "Tell me what you want," he groans, his mouth now nipping at my ear.

"More," I moan, my breath short. He obliges, and his thumb finally strokes my most sensitive spot, pulling a gasp out of me. His fingers curl inside, hitting every spot, and my breath hitches.

"God, you're driving me crazy," Logan gasps in my ear. My eyes flutter as my head rolls back, and I can't bring myself to speak, to tell him that he's the one who's driving me crazy with the circular motion of his fingers. He's building up the tempo, becoming a bit rougher now, and hearing his own breath hitch in my ear is enough to bring me over the edge.

Wave after wave of pleasure rolls through me; my legs shake, but he's holding me tight, nowhere close to letting me go. I catch myself screaming his name, and as I come down my high, he peppers my collarbone with gentle kisses.

I melt against him, positively boneless, and bask in the bliss he has brought me in this magical place.

Chapter 17

It's Saturday, and because I've made such good progress on the website, I decide to take the entire day off. During my last Zoom call with Leslie, she loved the new style. "Do more of *that*," she said. I just hope I can keep it up before I run out of steam.

This is Logan's day off as well, so he decides to take me to the Skyline Trailhead, one of the must-see areas of Cape Breton. The trailhead is one of many trails scattered around Cabot Trail, which surrounds the peak of Cape Breton like a ribbon. It's all winding roads and stunning cliffside views to get there, and I'm so excited to see Skyline that I barely even think about what's been on my mind recently.

Although Logan and I talk about pretty much everything, I've yet to crack the code on how to talk to him about his job. Not his summer job at the lodge, but his real job, the one in San Francisco for which he abandoned his home and family.

And now that my days at the resort are nearing their end, I'm starting to feel the pressure of what's next. It's creeping in slowly, more and more every day. After about a week of this routine, I know I need to crack him open and make some progress on this topic, or else I'm going to be stuck going back home without any answers.

And I can't have that.

"I just hope it's not too foggy today," Logan says as he's pulling into the parking area of Skyline Trail.

"It doesn't look foggy," I tell him, confused. As I get out of the car, I look around; sure, there are some clouds in the sky, but it's mostly sunny. There's no sign of any sort of fog.

"From here, it doesn't. But when we're up there ..." Logan points towards the forested area in front of us. That's where the trail begins. "We'll be high enough to dip into the clouds. And there are clouds today, so ..."

"Okay, that is so cool."

"It is, and it's pretty eerie, but when I came on my own, I almost didn't see anything at the top because of all the clouds." Logan peers towards the sky, shielding his eyes with his hand. "It doesn't look too bad right now. Maybe we'll get lucky." Then, he looks down at me and gives me one of his signature smiles. My insides go all gooey, and I reach to grab his hand.

The trail is nothing short of spectacular. And it's so different from yesterday's trek to the waterfalls. At first, it looks like any old trail in the woods; it's forested and shadowy, but the trees are short enough to let the sun through. But as we venture further into the trail and higher up in altitude, the trees begin to recede, letting way for open, mountainous plains.

Now I begin to see what Logan meant. Below the trail, the mountain dips down, but we can't see below; the clouds obscure the way. From here, it looks like thick fog. "There aren't as many clouds as when I was here last time," Logan explains. "I think that if we make it all the way to the top of the trail, we might see something more."

I look around, completely enamoured with the beauty of this place. I'm no stranger to wilderness trails. Growing up in Western Ontario meant I had plenty of those lying around. But this place feels so different. We're literally in the sky, above the clouds. Since the trees are sparse up here, the plains and mountains open up around us, displaying a lush landscape of colourful flowers and grass. I inhale deeply, awakening every sense I have. The scent is fresh, floral, and earthy.

"So, I need to know," I begin as we walk. "Did high school suck for you as much as it did for me?"

Logan visibly cringes. "Well, it wasn't *that* bad. Honestly, once we got to that point, I didn't really get bullied or anything. It's like people moved on and did their own thing. At least, that's what I did." He's got a thoughtful look in his eyes. "Not to say it was a great experience, either. It was really lonely. There were the jocks and the guys who were into literature … but I was pretty much the only computer-obsessed nerd at that school. At least for the cohort I was in. So I didn't even fit in with the other nerds." He chuckles. "But that's okay. I've always been fine on my own." Then he turns his neck to look at me and grabs my hand. "Although, I much prefer to be here with you. You're pretty much the only person I couldn't get tired of."

My heart skips a beat at the reminder that I matter to him. At the same time, my stomach drops a little. It sucks to know he was out there, all alone. Yet another reminder of the consequences of us moving away. Of me ghosting him.

If I'd kept talking to him, he could have had company, at least virtually.

I close my eyes for a moment and try to shake it off. I'm not going to sabotage myself. Not again. I told Sophie I could move past this. *Stop feeling guilty for what is already done.*

"I already know you just had Sophie," he continues. His hand squeezes mine as if to comfort me. "I can see why. You two are, like … the opposite of each other. She's like the extrovert that adopted you."

"Yeah, pretty much," I chuckle. Because that's exactly what happened.

"Did you …" He looks hesitant. "Did you have any boyfriends in high school?"

"A few, actually." But I don't want to go there. My chest feels heavy at the memory. The truth is, the few relationships I had with guys from my high school days weren't for the right reasons. Most of the time, I can't even remember what I saw in them. All that mattered to me back then was that they wanted me. And that was good enough for me.

Logan frowns but immediately tries to fix his expression. "Cool."

A giggle erupts out of me, and I pull his hand so he'll stop walking. "Are you … jealous?"

His eyebrows go up as if he's offended. "No! Well …"

"You are," I tease, giving him a playful poke in the belly. But I poke too hard and hurt my finger against the hardness of his abs. "Ow."

Now it's his turn to laugh; before I can react, his arms move toward me and pick me up over his shoulder. I squeal in delight.

"Okay, yes, thinking of other guys touching you makes me feel jealous. What can I say?" He laughs as he spins me around once. I squeal again, and he carefully lowers me down in front of him. I'm dizzy from being up in the air but also from being drunk on all of him.

He doesn't let me go when my feet hit the ground. Instead, his hands stay steady on my hips, the heat of his skin burning through the thin fabric of my legging shorts. He looks down at me with an intense twinkle in his eyes.

Logan moves one hand from my hip to my jaw; the soft contact ignites a thousand sparks within me. At that moment, I want to tell him the truth: I love him fiercely, with everything that I am and everything that I have.

But I can't. Not yet. I can't put all my cards on the table like this, not when I have no idea what he's got planned next. What if it scares him off? What if it's enough to make it all too much?

I can't have him leave, not like the others.

His thumb strokes my jaw. "Where did you go?" he whispers, kissing the sensitive spot below my ear.

"I'm right here with you," I whisper back before emitting a soft moan. My hands begin to travel around his back, just under the hem of his T-shirt.

"Hmm." I'm not sure if he's reacting to my touch or to what I said. I gasp when his teeth nibble at the spot where my neck and jaw meet. "You are now." His breath is hot against my neck. Pressure starts mounting in my belly. But too soon, he pulls his face away, not letting go of my cheek. I'm confronted by the worried look in his hazel eyes. "Everything okay?"

"Yes," I whisper in a pleading tone. I want his lips on me again.

He smiles. "Sorry if my boyfriend question made you go to a weird place."

It's my turn to smile. "Nah, right now you're all I can think about." His scent is intoxicating.

"God, I like the sound of that." He closes his eyes and takes a deep breath. "But, for the record, this trail is much more popular than the waterfalls. I don't think we can take that risk here."

"Oh." I drop my hands away from his back, unable to hide my disappointment. But he's right.

"Holy shit." Logan's mouth falls open. He points forward. "Look."

I twist to look where he's pointing, and it's my turn to gasp. It looks like we've made it to the top ... the clouds have cleared at some point during our embrace.

In front of us is the whole world.

I can't help but catch my breath as the land opens wide around me, a natural amphitheatre that's both wild and wondrous. My shoes clack against the old wooden platform above this cliff, a remnant that feels like a handshake between the world we know and the untamed. Below, the coastline snakes into the mainland, a dance of deep greens against the blue vastness of the sea that stretches out like a restless beast.

I squint up at the sky, a sprawling stretch of the softest blues scattered with clouds that hint at far-off places and the echoes of ancient storms. The sun's hanging up there, too, a generous dollop of gold, spilling its light all over the waves, making the whole ocean glint and gleam. The smell here—it's something else. It's like the sea and the pines are having their own kind of dance, twirling together and filling up my head with the kind of scent that makes you think of adventures.

It's quiet, a kind of silence you can't find just anywhere, a stillness that says this place hasn't been rushed by time or touched by too many footsteps. I stand there, letting myself just breathe it all in, thinking that maybe, just for a little while, I could just be a part of it all.

"Holy shit, indeed."

Logan steps onto the platform with me and gazes outward. I don't know how much time passes while we simply admire the view before us. It feels like a part of me is floating above it all, taking it in.

After a moment, I look at Logan, who's still gazing outward. Against this backdrop, I'm once again stunned that this man is real. Just looking at him makes my insides turn to mush. I have to concentrate to keep my knees from giving out. Somehow, I lucked out and got to have him in my life again.

And he wants me. This thoughtful, intelligent, kind, beautiful man wants me like I want him. My heart swells with the thought of it, so much so that I have to look away to keep my composure.

This is exactly why I have to get clarity on what happens next. Because I can't bear the thought of going back to how my life was before. I can't bear the thought of going home to my lonely apartment with too much time by myself to just think and get myself panicking. Now that I know what it is to live alongside Logan, that's all I want.

"I bet they don't have views like this in San Francisco," I begin, feeling my hands start to shake. I'm scared to venture here. But I have to.

"Actually, that's not quite true," Logan corrects me with a humorous look. Immediately, I realize how stupid my comment was. San Francisco is in California. Of course they have views like this. "But I'll be honest ... I didn't really make the most of it."

"Why not? You were quite the wilderness lover back in the day."

Right away, I can see I've said the wrong thing. His smile vanishes.

"Working at a startup is ... gruelling. So finding time to do that other stuff ..." His voice trails off. He's not speaking with his usual self-assured tone. It doesn't seem like he wants to dive deeper into the subject, but I have to know.

"Speaking of which, have you thought about what you're going to do? After the summer?" I take a deep breath. "I know you said you didn't know. But, as you probably know, my time here is coming to an end pretty soon, so I want to know where that leaves us. Should I be planning a move to San Francisco, or what?"

Logan is quiet for a moment. He doesn't look at me. "No, I don't think so."

My stomach sinks. I'm not sure whether he doesn't think so because he's not going back to San Francisco or because he doesn't want me there. "Oh. Okay. So, are you going to be working from home after this and moving back to Canada, or …" I trail off, hoping he's going to finish my sentence.

"I …" He looks down. With his face like this, I can't read his gaze. "I guess I'm still figuring it out."

"Okay, cool, cool," I say, trying to keep my voice steady. I can't figure out what's going on, and I don't want to come across as needy, but it comes out anyway. "Well, I'd love for you to keep me in the loop when you figure it out. Because, from where I'm standing, it certainly looks like you're treating this as a summer fling."

He jerks his head up at me. There's hurt in his eyes. "That's not it at all."

"Isn't it?" I cross my arms and try to keep breathing. The pitch of my voice is getting out of control. "Like I said, Logan, I've got, like, a week and a half left here. And just so we're crystal clear, in case I haven't made it obvious yet, I don't want this to be a summer fling."

There we go. I'm ready to lay my cards on the table.

"Logan, I'm ready to do the work to keep you in my life this time. I'm not going to flake and run away when it gets hard for me." Tears begin to fill my eyes, but I keep them down. I don't want to make a scene. "Because I am so, so sorry I abandoned you back then. I really am. I wish so hard I could take it back. But I can't. And this time, I don't want to walk out of your life. I'm serious. But I need to know what you want. Because I can't bear being abandoned again."

A look of confusion crosses his face. "Again?"

I immediately realize how this must have come off to him. How it seems like I'm blaming him for abandoning me when the opposite is true.

I don't have a choice anymore. I have to tell him. "My dad left."

"What?"

I rub my face with my palms. "He's out of the country. I know he's alive, but that's all I know. He's completely MIA. I thought I could rely on him, and I was wrong." I look up at him with fire in my eyes. "So I need to know if I can rely on you. Or if I should start preparing myself for another heartbreak."

He takes a deep breath. His eyes are dark and sad. "Shit, Avery. That's such a shitty thing for him to do. I'm so sorry." He rubs the back of his neck. "I do want you in my life, Avery. I don't want to abandon you. Far from it. And I believe you. And I don't hold what happened back then against you." He moves forward and wraps me in an embrace. His breath is hot against my neck. Everything feels a bit better here. "You were going through a lot. Your entire life got uprooted. Again. I'm just so disappointed I could do nothing to help you through it. And seeing how much you're going through again, there's nothing I want more than to help you this time around."

For a moment, we stand there in each other's arms. His scent blends with the smell of the outdoors in one soothing concoction. I wish I could bottle this up and put it on my pillow.

Still against my ear, Logan continues: "I've just got some shit I need to figure out before I can give you a clear answer. The last thing I want to do is lie. So I don't want to tell you anything I don't know."

I pull away just enough to look into his eyes. "What kind of shit?" I ask, hoping he will open up and tell me.

But instead, he only shakes his head. "I'll let you know when I know. I promise."

"I can help you figure it out," I continue. "If you're not sure what to do, or if it's got nothing to do with me … I'm here for you."

He just nods. "I know."

The conversation doesn't go any further than that. We make our way back, a bit more quietly than before. I can feel something is significantly different about the way he's walking, talking, and looking at me. And I just wish I could know what's on his mind so I can help him with it.

The evening ends as it always does—in my bed, the two of us coming undone together. I remain in his arms afterward, and just before I drift into sleep, I can't help but think everything's going to be okay after all.

But when I wake up the next morning, Logan is gone.

Chapter 18

Logan's side of the bed is cold. He's been gone for a while, then. Slightly panicked, I look around the cabin's only room, hoping he's just making coffee, or preparing breakfast, or taking a shower, or *something*.

The door to the bathroom is open, so he isn't there. And he isn't in the kitchen corner, either. I get up from the bed and slip on the closest piece of clothing I can find, then make my way outside to see if he's hanging out there.

Nothing.

I try to ignore the sinking feeling in my stomach. Maybe he just went to get us breakfast. But he's never done it without telling me first. He'll always kiss me awake and let me know where he's going. He has never just up and left without warning before.

Still, that could be it. Maybe he just wanted to let me sleep. I think back to the day of the storm out at sea, where he

let me sleep through dinner. The night we first had sex. I feel queasy with the mix of dread and fondness at the memory.

But this is probably just my anxiety trying to sabotage me again. There's most likely nothing to be worried about. Instead of falling prey to this feeling and diving deeper into my own thoughts, I do the logical thing and grab my phone.

I send Logan a text:

Hey, where did you go? I didn't get my good morning kiss.

There. He'll tell me what's up soon enough. While I give him time to respond, I scroll through social media to keep my brain distracted.

This is nothing. It's probably nothing. I always make a big deal out of tiny things, so this is just another of those instances, right?

That's got to be it.

That's got to be it.

That's got to be it.

Even though I try to keep myself distracted, I can't help but notice he hasn't responded yet. Maybe he's busy; if he's getting us breakfast, he might be grabbing everything and packing it up to bring back to my cabin. Or maybe he's talking to a colleague he met along the way. There are a thousand reasons he might have to not be able to instantly text me back. Most of these reasons having nothing to do with me.

I put my phone in my pocket and start walking. It's another beautiful day, with hardly a cloud in the sky. Once again, I'm stunned by the beauty of the ocean and the cliffs in front of me. So I walk along the side of the cliff until I reach our little bench. The same bench we've been sitting at every single evening.

I sit there and look out towards the ocean. *Think about anything else. Literally anything. Your client project. Your mom. God, even think about your dad.*

Unable to keep myself distracted, I take my phone out of my pocket and send another text:

You ok?

Then I place it back in my pocket, expecting to feel his response vibrate anytime soon.

Time goes by as I lose myself in the soothing rhythm of the waves below. The sun is beginning to get a bit too hot on my skin without any sunscreen, but still, I don't move. I stay there, mesmerized by the waves below me, because if I can lose myself like this, I don't have to be stuck in my head. I don't have to face the rising panic and dread that's starting to creep through my body like poisonous vines.

I'm brought out of my reverie when someone calls out from behind me: "Alone this morning?"

I turn to see an older woman with kind eyes and copper skin, probably in her mid-sixties, standing just behind my bench. I've seen her several times during the past few weeks at the resort; she's staying in one of the rooms at the lodge. Logan and I often see her eating lunch with her two friends—or two sisters, I'm not sure—while we're eating, too. We've shared a bit of small talk here and there, but nothing beyond that.

"Guess so," I say, trying to keep my voice from breaking.

"Where's that handsome fellow of yours, then?"

I feel a ball choke at my throat. I wish I could answer

her. Truth is, I have no idea where he is and why he won't respond. Because maybe it won't be okay. Maybe he got scared yesterday, and now I chased him away by pushing too hard on a subject he clearly wasn't ready to talk about.

But then again, if he's telling me the truth, why wouldn't he tell me all of it? It doesn't make any sense to me. I even offered to help. So if he didn't take the help, it has got to be about me. Why else would he do this?

"Oh, he's off working," I say instead, averting my eyes so she doesn't notice I'm lying.

"I see." She approaches and places her hand on the bench. "I hope you don't mind me saying this, but you two are such a beautiful couple. The way that young man looks at you ..." She sighs. "It's easy to see he's completely smitten by you."

"I don't know about that," I say without meaning to. I almost cover my mouth in embarrassment.

The woman looks at me, intrigued. "If you can't see it, you're blind as a bat, if you don't mind me saying."

"Maybe. I don't know." I sigh as well. "I'm sorry, I don't mean to be rude. I'm just a little anxious, is all." Understatement of the century. I'm hoping she'll take the hint and leave me alone. She's kind, but I don't have the emotional capacity to be around someone else and make small talk right now. To keep my mask up.

But she doesn't take the hint. Quite the opposite; she sits herself on the bench next to me. "You remind me a bit of myself at your age," she says with a kind smile. "I was a little ball of anxiety. Of course, that's not what they called it back then. My husband—God rest his soul—used to say

I would get hysterical." A look of horror appears on my face, but the woman chuckles. "No, not like that. He would say it in a loving way. Not in any sort of demeaning way. We just didn't have any other name for it. But he was always there for me, even when I had days—no, weeks— at a time where I couldn't leave the house."

She looks out at the ocean. "I was lucky enough to never be alone. I had my husband, and when he passed, I still had my dearest friends who understood me. Now, my wife is taking up this mantle." She chuckles. "Imagine that ... I got to find the love of my life, twice. But not everyone gets that luxury." She turns to look at me; her gaze is intense. "And when you find someone like that, someone who will stand by you, someone who understands ... The anxiety will try to take them from you. But you can't let it."

I slowly nod, suddenly feeling a wave of empathy for this woman. I can't imagine growing up forty years prior. And I feel an unbearable sadness at knowing her loving partner is gone. I know that part of growing old with someone means running the risk of outliving them. The logical side of my brain understands this. But I usually try not to think about it for more than a second because I know how much pain I can cause myself for something that is likely more than decades away.

When the woman eventually bids me goodbye, I make my way back to my cabin. On the way back, I try to call Logan instead of texting him. Even though I secretly hope for him to pick up, I'm not too surprised when it goes to voicemail after several rings. At least he hasn't blocked me. And seeing as it took a while before going to voicemail, he didn't see my name and deny the call. So maybe he really is just busy.

So I need to do the same and keep myself busy. It just so happens I've got work to do, so I take a quick shower before making myself some coffee and setting myself up with my laptop on the small porch outside.

The first thing I do is check my email. I sift through the first few, which are junk, but stop at one of the subject lines:

Inquiry about your website copywriting services

My heart starts pumping faster; this is good. This whole month, I haven't done any prospecting for myself, which means I have no more income lined up after the Panchakarma retreat project is done. And I haven't even given myself permission to worry about that just yet, so this is such a relief.

I open the email and read it over. It's from a man named Matt, who apparently heard about me from a past client of mine. He's interested in getting on a call with me at 'my earliest convenience' to discuss the relaunching of the website for his software company. *Perfect.* I type back a response and give him some availability for the next few days, then dive straight back into my copywriting work for my current project.

Knowing there's a high likelihood of a new gig awaiting me does ease some of the stress of whatever comes after this *workation*. If I can get this gig, it'll give me a cushion to pay my bills and afford some food while I work on securing more business in the upcoming months.

But I still don't know if I'll be doing it all alone or if Logan is part of that future.

After an hour of working, I look back at everything

I've written and wince. It's shit. I've been too distracted by wondering why I haven't heard back from Logan yet, and I just can't get in the flow. And Leslie has made it very clear that she expects the rest of the website to be on par with what I've delivered already. I can't achieve that level of quality without getting back into flow.

I sigh and close my laptop. It's no use. I've only got a bit of work left to do to complete the website, and it's definitely not happening today. At least, not until I hear back from Logan and know he's okay. That we're okay.

The last time I had doubts, Sophie talked me out of it. So that's what I need right now. A pep talk from Sophie. She'll help me remember that this isn't a big deal.

I put my laptop away inside and go sit on my patio again before dialling Sophie's number. Hopefully, the baby isn't napping, or at least, she's kept her phone on vibrate. I begin to wonder if I've made a mistake just as Sophie picks up.

"Hey!" she greets me. "Perfect timing. I'm nursing, so I needed to pass the time."

"Oh, well, that's just perfect, because I need to rant again and have your sage advice to stop me from spiralling."

"That's what I'm here for. What's up?"

I take a deep breath. "I think I fucked up yesterday. And now Logan left without waking me up and hasn't responded to my texts or calls."

"Dude, that's rude. He's straight up ghosting you?"

"Yeah. Either that, or he's busy." Or in trouble. But my gut tells me that's not it.

"Geez, what did you say to him? Did you actually fuck

up, or are you being too hard on yourself again?"

I sigh. "That's why I'm calling you. I was hoping you could tell me." I then tell her about our hike at the Skyline Trailhead and detail our conversation.

"Hmm," Sophie mutters.

"What?" Something about her tone is weird.

"Don't take this the wrong way," she starts. "And don't get me wrong, what he's doing right now is wrong. It's a complete overreaction. It's immature, and it's also not fair. Actually, it's unacceptable from a grown-ass adult. So he's being an idiot."

I sense a 'but' coming, so I grit my teeth in anticipation.

"But I've noticed you tend to do this often, Avery. And sometimes, it can kinda be a lot..."My stomach twists. "Do what?"

I hear her sigh on the other end of the line. "Based on what you just told me, he clearly said he had shit to deal with, and it seemed pretty obvious that he didn't want to talk about it. He's not ready. Even if you might feel like he should be, he's giving you all the signs that he isn't. And yet you kept pushing."

"I just want to help him through it," I argue. I can feel tension rise in my chest and through my fingertips. "How is that too much?" I try to keep control of my tone, but my voice is slowly rising.

"I said not to take it the wrong way," Sophie retorts. She sounds annoyed. "And I'm the one who's trying to help you right now. That's what you wanted, right?"

"And I'm trying to understand how it's too much." *How I'm too much.* "You were the one who said it was obvious he was in love with me. So if that's really true, why won't he accept my help?"

"That's the thing," Sophie says, sounding exasperated. "You're making a false assumption. He can be in love with you *and* want to be left alone with this issue. For crying out loud, Avery—you always do this."

"What are you talking about?" My pulse quickens, my breaths getting shorter and faster.

"You always assume it's your job to save people. It's not. I know it's hard, and I know the anxiety makes it harder, but seriously, just stop pushing so hard. Let things happen."

I'm about to boil over. "When have I done this?"

"You tried to do it with your mom when your dad left. You tried to do it with me when Matthew was coming on too hard right before we started dating. Sometimes all you need to do is be there for people instead of pushing to save them. I can even bet you're thinking of doing the same with your dad right now."

Anger spikes in my throat like a tidal wave; it consumes everything too quickly for me to mitigate what's about to happen.

"Fuck you," I spit back right before I hang up. A jolt goes through my entire body, and before I can hold back, I jump to my feet and throw the phone on my bed. It falls between my pillows.

The panic bursts and explodes into a million tiny shards across my body. But this time, I'm completely alone.

And it's my fault.

Chapter 19

The familiar crunching of gravel rouses me from my work. I lift my eyes from my laptop screen to see Logan walking up the path to my cabin, his shoulders hunched and his hands shoved in his pockets. His eyes meet mine through my open window, uncertainty swirling in the golden flecks of his hazel eyes before he gives me a tentative smile.

One week. It's been one week.

My heart leaps, but I force my expression to remain impassive. I've got my camera on, after all. I turn my attention back to my computer, trying to focus on the video call with Leslie. She's yet again gushing about the latest batch of pages I delivered for the retreat website.

"This part here really speaks to the tranquil vibe we're going for," she says, her voice alive with joy. "And the writing has so much more heart now. I can tell you really took the

time to understand our vision."

I'm only half-listening, hyperaware of Logan lingering in my peripheral vision. After a week of radio silence, what does he expect? That I'd welcome him back with open arms? That I'd drop a client call and leave everything behind to greet him? My fingers curl into fists as I struggle to rein in the storm brewing inside me.

Because I'm pissed.

I took the opportunity for this week to just focus on my work. I buried my feelings deep down to give myself a chance to finish this project with whatever steam I had left. I haven't texted my dad, or Sophie. I haven't even tried to contact Logan, no matter how much I desperately missed him with every fiber of my being. And I set my anger aside for both of them.

After all, I'm here to write. So that's what I've done all week.

I meet Logan's gaze again. He finally realizes that I'm on a call, so he stays outside instead of trying to come into the cabin. He gets settled on the picnic table, and I wonder how I'm going to bring my attention back to this call.

"—the next project. Would you like to talk about that?"

"Huh?" *Shit.* I must have missed something. "I'm sorry, could you repeat that? I lost you for a second." Ah, the joys of online communication.

Leslie doesn't skip a beat, nor does she seem to suspect I've just lied to her face. "The team really loves your work, Avery, so if you have some time, I would love to discuss another potential project we have in mind for you."

Oh, wow. Normally, I'd jump on this opportunity and say yes without hesitation. But I know there's no point in doing that right now. I'm not going to be remotely useful unless this freshly aroused anger dissipates.

So I lie again: "I've actually got another call booked in a few minutes, so I can't really stay. But I would love to discuss this further. Let's book a time for it; how about tomorrow at 1 p.m.?" I'm surprised at how professional and courteous I'm able to be.

We wrap up shortly after booking a follow-up call for tomorrow, and I close my laptop, eyes downcast. I take a deep breath in and exhale through my mouth before getting up to meet Logan outside.

I try not to storm out of the cabin, but it's hard to keep my cool. I remind myself of Sophie's voice, telling me to chill, but that only serves to remind me of how we left things the last time I called her.

Yeah, I'm on my own for this one.

I burst out of the cabin, breathless. Logan is sitting on the weathered picnic table, elbows on his knees, staring absently at the gravel. He looks up at my sudden exit, regret etched on his face. I open my mouth, ready to unleash a tirade of hurt and anger.

But then he's crossing the distance between us in quick strides. Strong arms envelop me before I can react, pressing me against his chest. Logan's familiar scent surrounds me, and despite myself, the fight drains out of my body.

It feels like I'm home.

"I'm so sorry," he murmurs, his breath warm against my

hair.

For a brief moment, I allow myself to melt into his embrace. I missed this so much. His scent, the warmth of his arms, just having him nearby. But the questions—and the anger—still plague my mind, threatening to spill. I pull back to meet his eyes.

"You can't just disappear for an entire week, ignore my texts and calls, and expect me not to be upset," I spit out, unable to keep the accusatory note from my voice.

He runs a hand through his dark curls. "You're right. That was shitty of me." His eyes are pleading for me to understand. "I swear, it's not what it looks like. I wasn't trying to ignore you or make you feel bad."

My expression must betray my skepticism because he hastily adds, "I'll explain everything, I promise. But I need to drive over to Sydney to pick up a custom set of bar glasses first. We're short-staffed right now, and after disappearing like I did, I kinda don't have a choice but to help out."

The thought of waiting hours more for an explanation makes my stomach churn. Being left in this unknown purgatory would surely drive me mad. I managed to keep it under for a week, although I still have no idea how I pulled that off, but now that he's back in front of me again, there's no putting that cat back into its bag.

I blurt out, "I'll come with you." Off Logan's surprised look, I add, "I can't just sit here wondering what happened. And we'll have plenty of time to talk in the car. This isn't a negotiation."

He considers this for a moment before nodding slowly.

"Okay then. If you're sure."

I give a terse smile. "Positive."

We waste no time getting into his car, which he parked next to my cabin instead of walking here. As Logan pulls out of the gravel lot, I see him shoot me a sidelong glance. There's a nervous energy thrumming under his composed exterior that sets me on edge. I brace myself for him to try and fill the painful silence, but he doesn't.

We drive in tense silence for a while before I finally speak up. "I still don't understand why you couldn't have shot me a simple text while dealing with whatever it was. Or answered my call. Or … something. It would have taken two seconds. And it wouldn't have let me believe you were ghosting me." I realize the irony of what I'm saying. If he wanted to be petty, he could tell me: *Now you know what it feels like.*

But Logan isn't petty. Instead, he sighs, his knuckles whitening on the steering wheel. "I know. You have every right to be upset. My mind was just … elsewhere."

I don't say anything, expecting him to continue. When he doesn't, I scratch my throat expectantly.

I'm trying to let the anger dissipate. He's here now, after all. That's what matters. Whatever it was, we can get past it. If we both want to. I need to give him a chance.

"Fuck, this is hard," he says as he grips the wheel even tighter. Outside the car, we're surrounded by the beautiful, winding cliffside landscapes of Cabot Trail. Under different circumstances, this drive could be a pretty cool date. "It's so difficult to explain. I don't even know where to start."

My stomach drops as I start to consider all the possibilities.

Give me uncertainty, and I'll give you back a thousand worst-case scenarios. "There's another woman?"

"What?" Logan is incredulous. He looks at me for just a moment, eyes wide, before turning back to the road. "No, that's … What on Earth gave you that idea?"

"Oh, I don't know, maybe the way you *disappeared* for a *whole* fucking week and ghosted me?" *Calm down, Avery.* My right hand is gripping the side of the cheap faux leather seat so hard I think my nails are going to pierce holes through it. "Is this payback for what I did?"

"No, absolutely not." Logan tightens his lips and raises his eyebrows. "And point taken." He shoots me a pained glance. "But I swear, that's not it. There's no one else, Avery. I get that you're angry, but frankly, is that what you really think of me? Do you really think I'd be capable of going to another woman just like that, after everything we …" he trails off and fixes his gaze back on the road. He's shaking his head.

"I honestly don't know. I don't know much of anything. I thought Jasper, my ex, wouldn't be capable of dumping me without giving me a good reason, and yet, he did." As soon as the words leave my mouth, I regret it.

Logan sighs. He sounds so tired. "See, what am I supposed to believe that you think of me when you compare me to your fucking ex, Avery?"

I shouldn't have said it, but it's beside the point. "You're trying to distract me from what you're actually supposed to be telling me," I say between gritted teeth. I just want him to explain. To give me a good reason that still allows me to stay in love with him without disrespecting myself.

"Okay, okay, fine." He takes another deep breath. "Sometimes I feel … off. I don't know exactly how to describe it. It's like whatever's fuelling me to do the basic shit we need to do, like getting up in the morning, going to work, talking to people, brushing your teeth, whatever … some days, it's just gone. I wake up empty."

The anger, which had previously been at a boiling point, suddenly cools down like I've been dunked into a frozen lake. Now we're getting somewhere. And it doesn't seem to be about me. He's telling me the truth.

"And some days things happen, and it makes it worse, and I just … I can't deal. With anything. So I run away. I turn myself off. It's so stupid …"

"It's not stupid." Calm has seeped back into my voice. I place my left hand on his thigh. Warmth erupts in my chest. I'm heartbroken by what he's feeling, but so overjoyed that he's sharing it with me. Maybe now I can help him. "So that's what happened? Something triggered you during our walk at Skyline, and … ?"

"Yeah. That's pretty much it." He stares ahead at the road. I take a moment to just breathe and take this in. What Logan just admitted to me feels uncannily like what I've been dealing with. That lack of inspiration, of energy to do what would normally be the easiest thing in the world. Like a light has been turned off inside you.

"Is that why you're here?" It has to be. We both have the same reason for being here. "You told me you needed to mix things up. So this summer job was to help you find inspiration again?"

"I guess so. I don't know." He shrugs. "I just know for a fact that ..." He raises his gaze to me. I want to kiss him so badly it hurts. "Being with you has helped. I've got fewer shitty days than ever before. Actually, every day I've shared with you has been better than what I could ever hope for by myself."

As much as this warms my heart, a thought occurs to me. I've come here to find inspiration again, sure. But I'm here doing work I actually enjoy. Writing, even if it's for other people like my clients, fuels me. It lights me up. It's my reason for getting up in the morning. "You know, it probably doesn't help that you're working here," I say before looking out the window at the stunning view. Clouds have started to form overhead, but it's beautiful nonetheless. Looks like it's going to rain.

"What do you mean?"

"I mean, I understand taking a summer to switch things up and coming here. It has worked like magic for me. And so has been spending my time with you." I shoot him a smile. "And I also know you need to pay the bills somehow, so I get taking the job. But ... haven't you considered this job might be making it worse?"

"I don't understand."

I sigh. "Back before I moved—when we were best friends—you were the smartest person I knew. But you were also at your best when working solo or with just me. You weren't a people person. So, take it for what you will, but I don't think working a customer-facing job in a resort is the best way to 'switch things up.'"

He frowns. "I disagree."

"Hear me out," I continue. "Logan, I know how you're feeling, okay? Shit, that's why I came here! You know that. But you're not going to get better by doing something that doesn't ignite your passion. That doesn't light you up. And this summer job obviously doesn't light you up."

"That's not true," he retorts, but his voice is calm.

"Isn't it?" I let out a frustrated sigh. How can I make him understand? "You're a genius, Logan. I can't stand to see you do this to yourself. That's one of the reasons I keep asking you when you're going back to your real job. Your programming job. I remember how much computer stuff would make you light up. You're not going to find inspiration and get that energy back without doing what you love. Don't you love it?"

"I do," he says sheepishly. "But—"

"And I also want to know because—and I thought I'd made this obvious—I want to tackle this next chapter with you. And I can't do that if I don't know what's next. And I'm glad you just told me everything because now I can help you through this. And if you want to change things up for real, maybe I can help you negotiate a work-from-home agreement with your job, and we can go somewhere, maybe we could travel to Europe, or Bali, or anywhere you want. I don't care where it is …" Shit, why can't I stop talking? "As long as we're both there, I really don't care, Logan, because I—"

"Avery, stop. Please stop." His tone is dry. Outside, it's starting to rain. Fog is beginning to creep through the peaks and valleys, obscuring the vistas.

"I'm not going to stop," I argue. My heart is going to beat

out of my chest. "You have a gift, and I'm telling you, if you don't use it, you're just going to keep being miserable and—"

"They fired me," he interrupts.

My blood goes cold. For a moment, I'm too stunned to speak. Then he continues. "I don't have a job to go back to in San Fransisco. I have nothing to go back to, in fact. I emptied out my apartment and brought everything back to Canada. I don't have a green card anymore without a job." He doesn't sound angry at me. He just sounds so … tired. "That call at the restaurant the other day? It was HR. They just needed some info to send me my final paycheck."

My heart hurts for him. I just wish he weren't driving so I could hold him and touch my lips to his. "That's so shitty," I start. "I'm so sorry to hear that, Logan. But you don't need to give up. There are plenty of other places that I'm sure will want your—"

"You wanna know the reason they fired me?" he bites back. "I've burnt out, Avery. And I wasn't getting better. The brutal deadlines, the ruthless competition, all the pressure? It drained every last bit of joy from coding. This resort job might not be glamorous, but at least I can breathe."

I go quiet, a little stunned. When I imagined Logan's programming career, I pictured fast-paced excitement, not soul-crushing stress.

I've been an idiot.

"I'm sorry, I didn't realize—"

The rain is coming down hard now, blurring the road ahead into a smudgy canvas. Logan's face is half cast in shadow, his eyes stormy. "Of course you didn't. This whole time you've just been trying to fix this instead of listening."

"That's not true," I argue. "I'm listening, Logan. I'm just trying to help—"

"I don't need your help!" he screams. "I'm not helpless, Avery. God. You always used to do this. You haven't changed."

My stomach feels full of lead. "What are you talking about?"

"You were always trying to defend me. Do you know how embarrassing it was to have a girl standing up for me in front of those immature bullies? Don't you think it made them want to bully me even more, thinking I couldn't stand up for myself? Did you ever consider that?" I've never seen Logan this angry. He's hardly ever angry in the first place. But now he's close to seething.

But I'm pretty close to it, too. "So, what did you want me to do? Leave them to beat you up? Just stand there like an idiot and do nothing? Just watch them hurt you? No way I was going to do that."

"I get that, but it wasn't your place," he bites back. "And neither is this. Whatever the way out of this burnout is for me, I don't need you to fix it. All I want is to have you here with me."

"But I can't stand to see you in pain!" I yell, a mix of anger and frustration. "If only you'd just let me help you see that you're not living up to your potential—"

"Please, *stop*," he says quietly, but firmly. "God ... is this why Jasper left you?"

Lightning goes through my chest. A tense beat passes. Logan exhales harshly, regret plain on his face. "Avery ... I didn't mean—"

"Stop the car," I choke out. We've entered the outskirts of a small town, and Logan pulls over to the curb.

"Avery, wait," Logan begs. "I'm so sorry—"

Before he can get another word out, I throw open the door and storm off into the rain, the panic clawing its way out of my throat with a scream.

Chapter 20

My breath comes in ragged gasps as I race blindly through the downpour. Fat raindrops pelt my skin, mixing with the hot tears streaming down my cheeks. Sobs threaten to rupture through my chest but get trapped in my tightening throat.

I'm spiralling, my vision blurring around the edges. It feels like hands are wrapped around my windpipe, squeezing until black spots dance across my eyes. I try desperately to get air into my burning lungs.

In my panic, I've lost all sense of direction. The quaint shopfronts have given way to a maze of narrow back alleys. I spot a darkened gap between two brick buildings and stumble into its refuge, my shoulders scraping the walls.

I sink down, heedless of the filthy puddle soaking through my clothes. Tremors wrack my soaked body as I hug my knees to my chest. I try to breathe, to grasp at any lifeline that could

pull me from this abyss of panic. But the same thoughts keep assaulting me like the endless rain.

You deserve this. You deserve this. You deserve this.

Logan's pained expression flashes behind my clenched eyelids. My chest constricts further at the memory of our fight, of the way I pushed him into lashing out.

He's right. This has to be why Jasper left. It's why Dad left. It's why no one wants you. It's why you're going to die alone.

I desperately long for the calming caress of fingers through my hair, for strong arms to anchor me against the storm raging inside. But I'm alone in this alley with only the cold indifference of brick and mortar bearing witness to my unravelling.

The panic rises, threatening to pull me under. I dig my fingernails into my palms, clinging to consciousness. But the walls seem to press closer, trapping me in this waking nightmare. My erratic wheezes echo mockingly back at me as I fight for air that won't come.

I claw desperately at my constricting throat, my ragged nails leaving angry red trails on my skin. I'm drowning on dry land. The world narrows down to my strained attempts to draw breath into my spasming lungs.

In some distant corner of my mind, I know I need to lower my heart rate. But crippling waves of panic continue battering me against the rocks, allowing no respite.

I squeeze my eyes shut against the vertiginous spinning of the alley. But instead of steadying darkness, vivid memories assault me. My dad's voicemail taunting me in the night. Jasper turning away with that last look of disappointment that shattered my heart. Logan's pained eyes as we exchanged cruel blows.

Oh God, Logan … A fresh wave of anguish washes over me. I'd give anything to rewind time and take back that entire conversation. Because despite our fight, there's nowhere in the world I feel safer than wrapped in his arms. No one who has ever come close to understanding the storms that rage inside me—except him.

But I destroyed that shelter, ruined that peace. Like I ruin everything.

And now he's going to leave me.

The crushing weight of this truth feels like concrete blocks piling upon my chest, pushing out the last bits of air. Spots burst across my vision, consciousness slipping from my grasp.

A small part of me wants nothing more than to let the darkness take over. To release the iron grip I still have on awareness and let the panic's riptide carry me under. Because it hurts. It hurts so fucking much I want to die in this moment.

But some primal instinct rebels against that fate. Through sheer force of will, I force myself to draw in a shuddering breath, then another. Each inhale fuels the dying embers of fight still left inside me.

As I cling stubbornly to consciousness, a sudden memory takes shape behind my closed lids. Thirteen-year-old Logan guiding me gently through the raging storm of my first panic attack. His voice a lifeline pulling me back from the brink, my hand clasped firmly in his.

In this moment, I need that Logan more than ever. But this time, I have no one to save me from myself.

As another tremor wracks my body, I know I can't endure this alone. My first instinct is to call Logan, to hear his soothing voice reminding me to just breathe. But the memory of our vitriolic fight still rings in my ears. After everything we flung at each other, I don't deserve his comfort right now.

My thumb hovers over my mom's number next. A wave of guilt washes over me. She worries so much. And she's happy now, finally past the way my dad left her. Do I really want to disturb that peace?

But the walls of the alley seem to creep closer with each ragged breath, reinforcing that I can't handle this on my own. With a resigned exhale, I grab my phone with trembling fingers.

Mom picks up on the second ring, her cheerful voice piercing through the deafening storm in my mind. "Avery! How are you, honey?"

Hearing the smile in her voice, I almost choke on the lump in my throat. She sounds so happy, oblivious to the darkness I'm about to drag her into.

"M-mom," I gasp out. I squeeze my eyes shut as if I can hide from the anxiety etched into that one word.

Silence on her end. When she speaks again, all traces of lightness have vanished. "Avery, what's wrong?" Tension vibrates through the phone line between us. "Talk to me. Are you hurt?"

I cling to the phone like a castaway to driftwood. But no words come out, just halting breaths that catch in my throat. I can picture Mom's face creasing in helpless worry at my silence. My chest constricts further, shame and panic swirling together in a toxic cocktail.

"I want to die, I want to die," is all that can come out of my mouth. "Mom, make it stop, please make it stop—" A scream erupts out of me. "No, no, no, no, no …"

"Avery, I'm here," I hear her say, but she might as well be on another planet. "Avery, listen to me. Listen to my voice. I'm here. Honey, my sweet girl, please, hear me. Mom is here …"

"Why did he leave?" The words come out strangled, half a scream, half a sob. "Why doesn't he love me?"

"Who? It's okay, honey, I'm here … I love you … so, so much …"

Another violent scream rips out of my chest. "He's gone, and he never loved me, did he, Mom? And no one ever will. It hurts, Mom, make it stop, it hurts, please, Mom, make it stop …"

I don't know how long I stay like this, with Mom whispering back to me in my ear, worlds away. I can hear her voice break, and know I've broken her heart because I'm so far away and there's nothing she can do while I'm begging her for help. And it makes it hurt all the more.

"I just want to die," I keep repeating, my voice getting weaker until they're no longer words—until whatever is coming out of my mouth means nothing except pain.

From afar, I can hear her voice telling me to breathe. It takes an eternity before I can listen, before my mind decides to obey and let my body know what to do. Slowly, breath by breath, I come back to myself, feeling my entire body tremble with the aftermath. I can hardly feel the wetness of the rain still pouring down on me.

"That's it," Mom continues. Somehow, her voice is clearer now, closer. "You're doing good, honey. Keep breathing. That's it."

My breaths are getting longer, deeper. And the storm that was screeching at full force in my mind begins to calm down. So does my heart. Ever so slowly, the panic dissipates, and I'm left with nothing but the stark melancholy of the aftermath.

I don't even hear his footsteps as he walks up to me. But he's there, crouching near me—he's real, and he's there, and he has found me. "Avery," Logan whispers, his eyes pained as he takes a good look at me. He turns his hand while his other arm wraps around my shoulders. "Hand me the phone."

Too stunned to argue, I take the phone away from my ear and hand it over to him. Logan sets it on his ear and doesn't waste a moment. "She's okay," he says, his voice a little unstable. "I've got her. She's not alone. She's going to be okay."

There's silence while, on the other line, I assume Mom asks who she's speaking to. Logan locks eyes with me and gives me a comforting smile. "It's Logan." More silence on the other end of the line. Then, I hear Mom's voice say something, and Logan repeats, "It's going to be okay. Hmm-mmm. Yes, I will. Okay." Then he puts the phone down, and his entire focus shifts to me.

"Avery, I'm here," he says right before trying to pull me up. "Let's get you in the car. It's getting cold." I let him manipulate my body into standing up, but my legs are so shaky I have to lean against him. My body hasn't fully recovered from this panic attack, and neither has my mind.

The rain keeps pouring down on us with no mercy. Now I'm starting to feel my body again, and Logan is right. It's cold. It's getting late.

I shiver against him.

"I can't apologize enough for what I said," he begins. His hand softly rubs my back. "I just want to be here for you, if you'll let me."

I'm no longer mad. I don't know how I feel. I'm just exhausted at this point. Instead of saying anything, I just nod, my head still leaning against his chest. He gets it, and he doesn't say another word until I'm safely tucked in his car, away from the rain.

When Logan is back in the driver's seat, he starts fiddling with the controls to get the car warmed up. "I wish I had a towel or something," he says as he looks at the back seat. "I guess I'd better just drive you back home and get you warmed up."

Tears well up in my eyes. These aren't the desperate sobs of the panic attack; they're the quieter aftermath of the wave of sorrow that always hits me after. "I'm so sorry, Logan," I begin. "About everything. About pushing too hard."

"No, no," Logan argues. He cups the side of my face, looks into my eyes, then gently puts his lips on mine. He kisses me softly, sweetly, and it makes my chest burn with regret for everything I've done.

Too soon, he pulls back without letting go of my face. "Don't worry about that right now. Who cares? I know I don't. Just focus on you. Keep taking deep breaths."

I listen to him and close my eyes as I keep breathing.

Deep breath in. Deep breath out. I fall into a rhythm, feeling his thumb stroke my cheek ever so softly.

I'm interrupted by my phone's ringtone. And I'm about to completely ignore it until something tells me to just *look*.

So I reach into my pocket and freeze when the word 'Dad' is reflected back at me.

Chapter 21

At first, I don't process it. I'm just staring back at my phone, unable to understand what exactly I'm looking at. The exhaustion has seeped deep into my bones, clouding my brain and my judgement.

I don't move. I don't breathe. All I'm able to do is stare.

A hand lands on my shoulder. Logan. I look at him, still feeling dazed and frozen in time. "Go ahead," he says, his voice so soft I can hardly hear. "I'm going to give you space, okay?" He looks at me expectantly, his eyes mellow and loving.

My hands shaking, I nod and look at the phone again. Suddenly, it hits me like a tidal wave, and I'm scared shitless. My entire body is on the edge of a crescendo, waiting for release. I don't know what kind of release it will be.

My finger hovers above the green icon. Logan smiles and exits the car. "I'll stay close," he whispers before shutting the door. And just like that, he's gone, leaving me alone in this

car, in the dark, to face the truth.

I pick up and place the phone against my ear. I open my mouth but can't bring myself to speak.

No words come from the other end, either. But I can hear stilted breathing. I'm not breathing. I'm holding it in, waiting for I don't even know what. My heart is beating a thousand miles a minute, so much so that my vision is getting blurry.

I finally allow myself to speak: "Dad?" The word comes out strangled. It's not my voice. It's someone else's body; I'm floating two feet above it, lost in a surreal mist of emotions threatening to tear me apart.

"Avery." It's him. It's his voice. I'd recognize that voice anywhere. It's on the phone, and it's more high-pitched than usual, on the verge of breaking, like mine—but it's him.

Two tidal waves collapse against each other within me; I don't know what I feel, but I feel it all. The dams break. I didn't know I still had any tears remaining in my body, but here they come, and I'm bawling like I've never bawled before.

I'm a child again; I've just clipped myself with a fishing lure, and it hurts, and he's there with me, hugging me tight, telling me I'm going to be okay. I'm five years old and crying against the airport window, happy tears warming my cheeks as I'm waving to Dad, who's getting out of the plane and coming home, he's coming home, he's …

HOME.

He's here.

He is here.

I can hear him on the other line. His short, heavy breaths, the sniffling, the sighs … and I know he's crying too. And for a moment, that's all we do. There are no words to be said. We simply sit here and listen to each other cry.

I didn't know it was possible to feel so many things at once. This makes panic attacks look like a cakewalk. I'm angry, relieved, melancholic, overjoyed, confused … Everything in my body burns. I yearn to scream at him and hug him through the phone and tell him I love him and tell him I hate him.

When I finally manage to speak, only two words make sense for me to say. "Why now?"

On the other end of the line, I can hear him taking a deep breath and trying to get a hold of himself. "Your mom called Andrea. Said to tell me that if I didn't call my daughter right this moment and make things right, she was buying a plane ticket to Colombia to kick my ass."

I laugh through the tears. Yet what he's just told me makes me feel even worse. "Why?" I repeat. And this time, I'm not asking why he's called me just now. He knows exactly what I'm asking.

He takes a deep sigh, and I hear him swallow back a sob. "Sorry doesn't even begin to cover it, Avery. I just … I don't know. I can't … I went off the deep end. I can't even begin to explain. Nothing would make this okay. I …" While he pauses, I close my eyes, letting more tears flutter down. "I don't know what's wrong with me. I fucked up, and I'm fucked up, and I don't know what happened, I just … fuck …"

"I needed you," I manage to say through my tears. "You don't know how much. You weren't there."

"I know," he replies. I can hear all the pain in his voice. I don't know if it makes me feel better or worse because I'm feeling it all at once. "I know that, and I'm going to regret that for the rest of my life. Please believe me when I say that."

There's more silence as we each sit here on our own side of the planet, processing the last few minutes. So few words have been exchanged so far, but to me, it feels like everything. It feels like a ton of bricks, and it feels like salvation at the same time.

"All I know is, I haven't been well, and no matter how many times I willed myself to call back, to even send you a single text, or to even read anything you sent to me or Andrea, I ... I couldn't. The last thing I ever wanted was to hurt you—the very last thing."

"But you did," I whisper. I can't get any anger to come out, though. I'm just deeply, deeply sad.

"I know. Oh, how I know, honey. And I never wanted you to see me like this. I never wanted you to have to see me brought down to this level. This is all me, Avery. It has nothing to do with you ... I didn't want this for you ... it's all me."

Now, I'm able to muster some anger. "But why?" I'm reminded of every time Dad was ever sick or unwell. Whenever it happened, I could barely catch a glimpse of him. He would hide out in his room, away from our prying eyes. And the one time I tried to make him chicken soup from scratch to help him feel better, he got upset. Said he didn't want me to have to care for him.

So I know that's how he is. I've known for a long time. And it hits me that this may be why he left us.

But it doesn't mean I accept it. "Why won't you let me in?

Why won't you let me help?"

"It's not your responsibility," he says in a tired voice. "It never was. I'm your father. I never wanted you to have to endure me at my worst ... or worse, have to take care of me. That should be my job, not yours."

"Dad," I say, swallowing back tears. "I'd rather endure you at your worst than not see you at all."

He stifles back a sob. "But this is what you do, my strong girl. You take in the worst of people onto yourself. And I can't let you do that. Not for me. I don't deserve it. I cannot watch you pour so much of yourself into helping me. I've watched you do it over and over again, and every time, you come back wounded. I can't be the cause of that."

"What do you mean?"

"You give too much of yourself to those who don't deserve it. That man, Jasper ... he never deserved everything you poured into him. You run yourself ragged trying to fix people, Avery. And I know you know this by now, but it only results in pain."

I take a moment to feel this deep within myself. A thousand stab wounds are ripping me apart from the inside.

"I just wanted to be worthy of him," I cry out. "Worthy of you."

"Oh, my strong girl," he says, sighing. "I've done you so wrong. You've always been more than worthy. You can't believe how proud I am of you. How much I love you. You do your best in everything, and I am so incredibly proud to be your father."

I need another break to let more tears out. I feel like the

entire ocean is flooding out of me, like there will never be an end to this.

He takes this chance to continue: "You don't need to fix everyone to be worthy, my strong girl. What I've been going through, what's been happening to me … It's my own doing. I've done things, I've pushed all of you away. Your mom, and now you … and I've got regrets, but I have to live with them. I have to process this. It's my problem. It's not yours to fix. The last thing I wanted was to bring you down with me. The last thing I wanted was to hurt you. There's not enough time left on this Earth for me to apologize enough for hurting you."

"I hear that," I manage to say. "But still, Dad … I needed you. Right now, everything's fucked, and everything hurts, and you weren't there."

"This is never going to happen again," he starts. "No matter what I'm going through, I'm going to be there for you from now on, I promise—"

"No." My voice is loud and clear. Almost panicked. "Don't you dare." I remind myself that I'm allowed to be angry. I picture Sophie in my mind. What would she tell me to say? "Dad, I love you. You know I do. I've never not loved you. But I'm so sick of being let down. I'm tired of holding out for a promise, of hoping you'll show up, and then having to deal with the disappointment when you don't." There's a sour taste in my mouth as I remember my seventh-grade graduation party.

My throat feels so heavy it's difficult to speak. These words hurt to say, but they're necessary. "I don't blame you. You've always provided for Mom and me. And I'm grateful for that … I really am. But whenever I needed you the most, you weren't there. I didn't just need a Dad with a good job, I needed a Dad who was there."

My words hang in the silence. I can hear his breathing picking up right up until his sobs come back. They rip through me like a hot blade. "I'm sorry," he repeats, over and over and over again. I don't say anything; I only listen and let my tears fall silently, my eyes closed. We're worlds apart, but in this moment, it feels like we're in the same room. In the same car.

"Okay," he finally manages to say. "You're right, my strong girl. I won't make any more promises. If that's what you need from me, that's what I'm going to do."

"Good." I wipe my face.

"And from now on, if you call or text, I'll do my best to answer. I won't promise I'll answer every time … but I will get back to you. I'm not going to do this again."

The storm is starting to subside. I take a deep breath, and I realize, in that moment, that I'm going to be okay.

It hurts, and my mind feels like it's been hit by a truck and thrown into a woodchipper, but I'm going to be okay.

"I'll be okay," I repeat out loud. "I want you to know that, Dad. I'm going to be okay."

"Of course you will," he says, his voice still shaking. "You're my strong girl. I never doubted you."

"But I need to figure my shit out," I continue. "Like you, I guess. And I don't think that's something anyone else can do for me."

He's silent, waiting for me to continue.

"I'm happy to know you'll try your best to pick up if I

call you. But … I don't think I should be calling you for a while. I'm not …" I take another deep breath. "I'm not mad anymore. I don't hold it against you. I just …" I try to find the right words. "I need to focus on fixing myself before I put any energy into fixing this. Fixing us."

"You're right," he replies. His voice is heavy. "And that's what I wanted for you in the first place. I want you to focus on yourself. Focus on being the best you that I know you can be, without having to worry about me."

Part of me does want to worry about him. Whatever he's going through all the way over there, he's still going through it. And so I wish I could put in the energy to start talking to him again, to begin to mend whatever has broken during all these months of silence. But I know I can't do that now. It may come later, but not now.

"I just don't want to hurt anyone," I say. I don't say the rest of the sentence:

Like you did to me.

"That's okay. You'll be okay." His voice is soft against my ear. "I love you, Avery. More than anything. More than I'll ever be able to truly show you."

"I love you too, Dad." A final tear escapes my eyes. I don't know how to end this conversation, especially since I don't know when we'll speak again. "Take care of yourself for me, okay?" It's the best I can do.

"I'll do my best," he says. "And you do the same, my strong girl."

"Okay."

I take the phone away from my ear, shoot one last look

at Dad's name on the screen, and close my eyes as I press the red icon.

My heart has shattered into a million pieces. I don't think I've ever been this exhausted. Despite all that, I see everything with crystal clarity. I feel calm and collected, like the sea after a devastating storm.

I know what I have to do now.

I'm going to have to break Logan's heart.

Chapter 22

It doesn't take too long before I hear tapping on the driver's side window. I peer over and see Logan looking inside. He's soaking wet. Now that I'm coming down from this emotional rollercoaster, I realize that I am, too. And I'm starting to feel the cold.

"You can come in," I say, hopefully loud enough that he can hear me, but my voice feels hoarse. Luckily, Logan nods and comes inside. His dark brown curls have been flatted against his head and face—that's how long he's been standing out in the rain. His clothes are soaked to the bone, so much so that I can see the outline of his muscles underneath the fabric.

There's a pang in my chest. God, he's so beautiful. And he's looking at me like I'm the most precious thing in the world, and I'm about to disappear into the wind.

Which, for all intents and purposes, I am.

He opens his mouth, but closes it, his eyes thoughtful. He

then repeats the motion and finally says:

"Do you want to talk about it?"

His thoughtfulness stings. Knowing what I have to do is torture. But not now. For now, I just need a rest. "I don't want to talk about it yet," I say. "But I do want you here. Can you just … be here with me and not ask?" There's a pang in my heart when I realize this is what Logan needed from me before.

He nods, giving me a smile, then grabs my hand with both of his and looks deep into my eyes. "I'm here. Okay?"

I'm all out of tears by now. I simply look back at him and nod. "Okay."

Logan lets go of my hand and starts the car, then turns on the heat. I'm shivering and surprised he isn't, although it might not just be the cold that's doing this to my body. I feel like I've just been swallowed and chewed back out.

So we start the drive back home in silence, exactly how I wanted it to be. I don't sleep, but I do rest my eyes. Even though it's dark out, and the clouds shield the sky so that even the moon doesn't shine through, the little light that remains in the world feels like too much to process.

Because I've got a lot more to process.

And it hurts that it feels so right. The way we're both silent but able to hold comfort in this silence. The way he'll occasionally glance back at me with a worried smile. The way I want to tell him to stop the car so I can kiss him, taste his mouth, strip him of these soaked clothes …

It's all too much.

But Sophie and my dad are right. It's not that I don't

deserve this. For once in my life, I truly feel like I do. Like I'm worthy of Logan. Like I deserve to be happy despite everything I've done. And maybe one day, I can have it all.

But not today.

The rain begins to slow down. Before we've arrived back at the resort, some of the clouds have cleared, giving way to the moon at last. But now I can open my eyes. I'm not feeling my best. Not even close. I'll need twelve hours of sleep or more to recover from everything I've been through today. But I'm beginning to feel human again. Whole again.

And that's a start.

Logan pulls into the resort and makes his way directly to my cabin. The closer we get, the more the anticipation starts biting at my heels. I don't want to do this. I want to say 'fuck it' and do what I feel like doing. But it wouldn't be fair. It wouldn't be fair to me, and it wouldn't be fair to Logan.

My heart's drumming against my chest when he pulls up at my cabin. There we go. We're here. By now I've stopped shivering, but I'm still cold and uncomfortable in my wet clothes, and despite everything else, I'm craving the comfort of warm, dry fabric against my skin.

Logan stops the car. He looks at me, his gaze intense, his eyes dark. "Let's get you warmed up," he whispers.

My lower belly tightens at his words. There's a part of me that wants to be selfish, that wants to take advantage of this moment and fall into bed with him. But I'm not going to do that. I'm not going to ignore everything else at the top of my mind and take advantage of Logan like that. That's not who I am.

"Maybe you should drop me here and grab some dry clothes at your place and come back after," I suggest while my hand grabs the door handle.

"I'm going to be okay," Logan responds. "I ... I don't want to leave you alone. Not like this."

I take a deep breath. Maybe he's right. I'd been hoping to extend this moment a little longer. To delay the inevitable. "Okay," I say, then open the door to make my way into the cabin.

Logan follows closely behind me. I unlock the door, my hands trembling slightly, and enter without a word. I remove my shoes and make my way to the bed at the center to sit on it as casually as I can.

Logan follows me with his gaze, then imitates me. Soon, he's next to me, and I can feel the warmth of his body tantalizing mine. How sweet it would be, how delicious, to have his chest against mine, for our skin to mingle and become one.

I look up at him and sweep a bit of hair stuck against his glasses. "Logan ..." I whisper, feeling my chest burn with both pain and desire at once.

Logan's hand meets mine. "Avery, I have to apologize. What I said back there ..." His eyes look down. "It was completely out of line. And I didn't mean it."

I give him a sad smile. "Logan, it's okay."

"It's not okay," he continues. "Because you were right, and that struck a nerve, and I lashed out at you for it. You're right that I should go back to what I love doing. I'm just ... scared." A sigh comes out of him, as if he had been holding it in for a long, long time. "No, I'm terrified. I'm terrified to feel these things again. To feel ... that fatigue, the soul-sucking exhaustion that tears everything apart. I would do anything not to feel that again."

I begin to stroke his back. I know exactly what he means because I have the same fear. I'm finally starting to feel like I've crawled out of whatever hole I was stuck in, and I don't ever want to slip back into that hole again. It's a hole that feels like death. I'd do anything to avoid it.

Which is why I have to do what I have to do.

"I know," I tell him, and before I can resist the urge, I lean my head against his chest. The sound of his heart beating soothes me. It's going to be okay. "And it's okay. I mean, I'm not angry. I don't think I could ever stay angry at you." I look back at him and brace myself to finally utter the words I've been meaning to tell him. "I love you, Logan."

There's a stunned look on his face for a moment as his brain registers what I've just said. I know he'll probably want to say something, but I take advantage of his silence to keep going. "And I think I always have. At least, as long as I possibly could. We were so young when we met, and this thing, this love, I think it slowly took root and bloomed over time, but it never left. It only grew with time. Even for all the years we were apart, there wasn't a single day you didn't pop up in my mind. I didn't realize it during that time, the way I thought about you, but that's what it was. It was love. *Is* love.

"And I want you to know that, Logan." My hand cups the side of his face. "I want you to know, before I say what I'm going to say, that I do love you, and I don't think that's ever going to change."

"Avery," he says, and before I can stop him, his mouth is against mine, sighing with relief. I can't stop myself from yielding to him, from opening my lips to him. He tastes like the rain, like salt and tears, and I never want to pull away. But too soon, he does. And his forehead presses against mine, like he needs more, like he's in pain. "I love you too," he responds, his breath heavy.

Part of me knew—no—all of me knew at this point. Whatever part of me denied he loved me was the same part that doubted I deserved it. But I'd be stupid to say I didn't know. Still, it doesn't hurt any less. Because now I have the confirmation that I'm going to break this heart.

"And I think I feel the same," he continues. "This thing between us, it's always been there. So much so that …" He pauses and takes a deep breath. "There hasn't really been anyone else. Not in any serious way, at least."

"Oh, Logan," I whisper, feeling a twinge of sorrow for him. How lonely it must have been.

"No one else ever really interested me. They all paled in comparison to you."

"Logan …" I slowly move away from him without getting too far, either. "I didn't lie before. I do love you. But …" His eyes shift. He looks scared. "When I first came here, I came to be alone. The way Jasper left, and then my dad … I needed space to think. And I needed it away from everyone else I knew. I also needed to write that stupid website, which I was able to do, in part thanks to you." I stroke his face with a sad smile. "And I'm so thankful I got to find you again. But through all of this … I didn't get to do what I truly came here for."

"Being alone," Logan finishes for me. Hurt flashes through his eyes, but he doesn't seem angry or upset.

"I know you apologized and said you were out of line," I begin, feeling my heart tear into a million little pieces. "But I think you were still right with what you said to me earlier tonight." And Sophie was right, too. So was my dad. "I push too hard to fix other people's problems. I'm so uncomfortable with the idea of other people being uncomfortable that I can't help myself. And I don't think …" I close my eyes and take a deep breath to steady myself. "I don't want this to erode the love between us. I don't want to hurt you again."

"You didn't hurt me," Logan interjects. "I'm not …" He swallows. "I'm not trying to talk you out of whatever you're trying to say. But I just want you to know, you didn't hurt me."

"But I could. Or this could build into resentment. Or something else. I don't know." I sigh. "The truth is, I think we both have some shit to figure out. And I don't want to speak for you. But on my side of things …" I need to say it. It needs to come out. "I think I need some time alone. To get some perspective. I need to heal without relying on someone else to do it for me." I look into his eyes, which have become glassy. The last thing I want is to make him cry. "And, like I said, I think you need this time, too."

"What are you saying, exactly?" he asks, his voice deep and heavy.

"I'm saying I desperately want to be a part of your life. But not now."

There. I've said it. In no uncertain terms. I close my eyes and feel everything shattering within me. Because I've spoken the truth, I desperately want to stay by Logan's side. One part of me—no, most of me—is screaming in horror at the idea of letting him go yet again. She's banging against the door, sobbing, pleading for me to stop this insanity as I set fire to her house. And I can hear her now, coughing against the smoke, screaming inhuman sounds as she burns.

That's how much it hurts.

But the other part of me knows I can be a better person. I'm already worthy of happiness, and I even think I'm worthy of Logan in a small way. But I don't want the bare minimum. I want to be the best possible person I can be for him.

Honestly, it feels like the least selfish thing I can do. Because when our paths cross again, I'll be the version of myself that can truly support him, no matter what he's going through. I'll be the Avery who is confident, stable—or at least partially stable—and who is capable of feeling whole and complete, even on her own.

That Avery will be so much better than this current version of me. The version who's still struggling to balance meeting her own needs and the needs of the ones she loves. The version who doesn't feel whole without another person by her side. This Avery is broken, and I need to fix her before I try to rely on Logan—or anyone else, for that matter.

But because she's broken, this hurts all the more. Because she's screaming at me to tell Logan I'm not going anywhere. That I don't want to spend a single day away from him, no matter where we decide to go.

A single tear falls from Logan's eye. I wipe at it with my thumb. Despite being all cried out, a tear escapes from my eye, too. "If you believe this is what you need," he begins, "I will give it to you. Because I already told you what I want. I want you to have everything you want."

His words tear through my heart. *I want you.* But not now. I have to be strong. To stop myself from saying those three words, I lean in to kiss him instead.

He kisses me back with urgency; his arms press against my back to pull me close. His tongue pushes my mouth open, and soon enough I have my own hands all over him, desperately clawing to hold on to whatever I can have. We're still in our rain-soaked clothes. Without any gentleness or care, I start peeling off his shirt to feel the cool, wet skin underneath. Soon enough, we're skin-to-skin, and the air is cold against us, but he's warm, and I'm warm, and we come together in a desperate tandem, letting tears freely flow.

It's a bittersweet goodbye, and it both hurts and relieves.

We lay in my bed after, warm under the blankets. My head is on his chest, and I hear his heartbeat starting to slow down. His fingers weave through my hair. I never want this moment to end. I never want morning to come.

"For the record," Logan begins, a slight crack in his voice, "I still feel incredibly lucky, despite everything."

"How come?"

"All this time, I've loved you. And I never knew if I could ever tell you. Because I didn't really think you loved me back. Not like this. I didn't imagine someone could love me like this."

My heart swells and screams all at once. "I did," I whisper against his chest. "I really did. I do."

Chapter 23

'm staring at my screen, still not 100 percent sure I clearly understood what Leslie just said to me. "I'm sorry, what?" It's only been a few days since I've been back home to my apartment, and my mind is still too busy replaying the breakup over and over to focus on anything else.

"Avery, your writing is nothing short of genius. Don't look so surprised! We'd be lucky to have you on retainer." Leslie's eyes are sparkling with excitement.

"I ..." I knew I'd nailed it, but this is much more than I'd expected. "I would love to, Leslie."

"Oh, and you absolutely must come to experience the retreat yourself," she continues.

My heart skips a beat. "Really?"

"Of course! If you're going to be writing for us long-term, you're worth the investment, darling."

"I'd love to," I reply, my voice meek. I'm trying to sound

grateful for the opportunity. But I'm out of money. There's no way I can pay for airfare to get there.

How can I tell her that without sounding completely pathetic?

"But it might be a little difficult, what with the—"

"Nonsense," she interrupts, a big smile on her face. "Since you'll be writing more content for us, it only makes sense for you to truly experience everything Prakriti Mountain Wellness has to offer. It's our responsibility to help you go through the experience."

"What are you saying?" I don't dare hope she's saying what I think she's saying.

"I'm saying we'll be sponsoring the trip."

I don't know how to feel. First off, it seems too good to be true. I'm still reeling from heartbreak and barely holding it together, so I dare not hope. This stupid apartment just doesn't feel like home anymore. This was Jasper's home. Another life entirely. The last thing I want is to be here, alone ... despite telling Logan I want to be alone.

But now I'm being given a second chance at a retreat. A chance to heal.

I explode into tears, unable to hold back. And I can't help the shame that crawls into my stomach. This is completely unprofessional of me.

But before I can explain myself or apologize, Leslie chimes in:

"And it looks like you'll be needing it, too."

"You have no idea," I say through my tears.

—

By the next morning, I've got a plane ticket booked for North Carolina that's leaving in two days. But I can't leave just yet. I still have one piece of unfinished business. So I swallow my pride and text Sophie.

I've been a major jerk and I'm sorry. I'm back in town. Can we please talk?

I crash on my couch and stare out the window while hopefully waiting for her reply. The office building staring back at me is still the same as ever. Like always, I can see the workaholic who's almost always in his office. He's still hunched over like he's starting to morph into his desk.

It's so weird. It really feels like nothing has changed. But I'm so bruised and battered that, in another way, everything is different. I have absolutely no idea where to even begin with myself now that I've made it clear I want to heal.

I do have one thing going for me—I know exactly what to expect when I land in the Blue Ridge Mountains. I've spent so long writing about it that I know everything I need to know about the Panchakarma cleanse I'll soon get to experience.

My phone vibrates against my thigh, and my heart skips a beat. I look at the screen and immediately sigh in relief at the sight of Sophie's name.

Was about time you came back. Come on over in like an hour or so. Heather's sleeping.

My heart leaps in my throat. I can't leave Montreal again without speaking to Sophie. Not only do I want to apologize in person for cursing her out when she was right about me, but I have to let her know what I've done.

I hope she's going to be proud of me. I know she wants me to allow myself to be happy, and this healing journey is the first step to making it happen.

Within the next hour and a half, I'm dressed and already knocking at Sophie's door in the Verdun neighbourhood. Her house is pretty close to the canal, and for a city house, it has a pretty sizeable yard. From what I can hear, Gwen is already out playing in said yard; I hear her squeal and laugh, followed by Matthew's booming voice.

My heart constricts, and I close my eyes. But I don't let myself get too envious. This could be mine soon enough. Once I figure myself out, if Logan doesn't find anyone else in the meantime, maybe this could be us someday. Maybe, in a few years, it could be the sound of our children laughing that I'll be hearing behind our home. But I can't expect him to wait around for me forever.

The door opens, revealing Sophie in a silk bathrobe with Heather in her arms. At first, I don't move or say anything; I simply stand there like an idiot, my mouth agape. But Sophie doesn't waste a second. She closes the space between us and wraps me in an embrace, and I find myself pressed against her and her tiny little girl. This contact brings me more comfort than I thought possible.

"I'm so sorry," I whisper against her shoulder. Heather coos, and I step back to give her some breathing room. This lets me look into Sophie's eyes so I can apologize properly. "I'm really sorry, Sophie. You were right. And I shouldn't have—"

"Don't worry about it. It's part of the job description." She smiles as she pulls me inside. "Come!"

An upbeat Sophie drags me through her kitchen and living room all the way to the porch in her backyard. When Gwen sees me, she stops the roughhousing with her dad and squeals my name before running towards us.

"Come here, you," I say as I catch her in my arms with a big hug. I hold her tight against me. There's nothing better than a toddler's hug.

"Aunty Avy, I learn how to do somersaults," she exclaims as she pulls away from my hug. Her eyes are bright with pride. "Come see, come see!"

"Wait a minute, Gwen, let's let Auntie Avery settle in first, okay?" Sophie calls out as she settles in at the large glass table on the porch. She's holding Heather against her chest.

"No, no, I want to see," I insist. I let Gwen pull me by the hand into the grass, where Matthew is still sitting with an amused look.

"Good to see you, Avery," he says with a wave. I respond with a nod and a big smile.

"Look, look!" Gwen lets go of my hand and proceeds to perform her somersault in the grass.

"Wow, good job!" I can't help the huge smile on my face. "That was so good!"

"Do you wanna play with me and Daddy?"

I shoot a look over at Sophie. I do, in fact, want to play with her, but the urge to have my conversation with Sophie is much stronger. Luckily, Sophie gives me a smirk before addressing her daughter: "Maybe a bit later, but for now

Auntie Avery wants to talk with Mommy, okay?"

Gwen pouts but immediately runs back to her dad as if she's completely forgotten about me. It's so impressive how quickly little kids can move on. They feel deeply, and sometimes in explosive ways, but they can bounce back from it all within minutes, if not seconds. I would be lying if I said I didn't envy it.

I head back to the table and sit next to Sophie. "Here, why don't you hold her while I get us some lemonade?" She hands Heather to me. I happily take her in my arms and gasp when she gives me a gummy smile. "Oh, aren't I the luckiest girl," I coo to her. She squeals in delight.

Sophie comes back shortly with two tall glasses of lemonade. "She's been smiling more and more often," she explains as she sits down. "I thought Gwen was a ray of sunshine, but this one? She's just always smiling now. We're so lucky." I watch Sophie's eyes fill with love as she looks at her daughter in my arms.

"I love her so much," I add as I start bouncing her on my knee a bit. "I missed them. I didn't think I'd miss them like this."

"I missed you, too," she replies before taking a sip of lemonade. "And I need to apologize to you, too."

"What for?"

"For not getting in touch after you …" She winces. "You know."

"You don't need to apologize for that.". My cheeks go pink with embarrassment. "You must have been pretty mad."

"Actually, no." She purses her lips. "I mean, sure, I was

angry at first. Like, my initial reaction was being angry. But after five minutes, I calmed down and figured that you needed some space. I knew you'd reach back out when you were ready, and I didn't want to push you. But I'm sorry if that's not what you needed."

"No, no, it's fine. I think it's exactly what I needed. In fact—" I inhale deeply, "that's what I told Logan, too."

Sophie frowns. "What do you mean?"

I proceed to tell her the whole story. The way Logan and I argued. His hurtful comment. How my dad called. And what I figured out I needed after all this.

Sophie sits there, looking dumbfounded. "So after all that … you broke it off? The guy told you he loved you—which, by the way, I told you so—and you decided to break it off?"

"Yes, because you were right," I say sheepishly. I stroke Heather's soft head; the gesture is more to soothe myself than her. "That argument was going to be the first of many. I don't want him to start resenting me because of my issues. I need to be alone. Like, really be alone and clear all this stuff out of my head. God, Sophie, I think it was the most painful thing I've ever done, but I think it's for the best."

She keeps staring at me with her mouth slightly open. "Still … I mean …" She sighs. "But if you're telling me that's what you need, then I believe you. It's just …" She pauses, and I can see her thinking hard. "Hmm."

"What is it?"

"Nah. Never mind." She shrugs and looks over at her partner and daughter. "So what now, then? It's not like you can afford another retreat."

I grin. "Yeah, about that …"

Chapter 24

'm sitting on the cobblestone deck overlooking the Blue Ridge Mountains, a blanket wrapped around my shoulders. The fire at the center of the deck is burning bright against the backdrop of the setting sun. I'm feeling a bit too hot—to be honest, the blanket is more for warmth than comfort. There's no need for blankets during a North Carolina summer night.

I'm far from alone. Around the fire sit half a dozen other people from all walks of life. Right now, they're chatting and laughing together. Normally, I would have joined them like I have for every previous night of my stay at Prakriti Mountain Wellness, but my mind is feeling a little distant tonight. Maybe it has something to do with the fact that we're all going home in the morning.

To say Sophie had been jealous was an understatement. After telling her where I was headed, I then promised I'd

check in after this extra project, after I'd racked up a bit more goodwill, to see if I could get a friends and family discount for her to attend the retreat. That satisfied her.

Now that the ten days of Panchakarma are over, all I can do is stare into the fire as the voices of my fellow retreat-goers ring in the background. The flames dance in harmony, bringing my heart along with it.

These past ten days have been nothing short of transformative. Everything I wrote about is true. I laughed, I cried, I dug deep in places I never thought I'd go. And now that it's all over, I'm trying to make sense of where I'm at.

Because, yes—I feel completely renewed. I feel like I've shed this skin and gone through a complete metamorphosis of the body and mind. Spending all this time alone but not alone, surrounded by the healers who held my hand all the way through, helped me kickstart the healing process. But now that it's all over, I can't help but feel like something is slightly off.

I don't know what I'm waiting for, exactly. Maybe it's time that needs to pass, to soothe my wounds. Maybe I'm still too close to everything. But part of me still feels heartsick. In my journey of healing and figuring myself out, I hadn't considered I would need to heal from this heartbreak. But of course, it's all part of it.

"Avery, you're awfully quiet tonight," one of the women, Yvonne, calls out to me. She's in her late sixties with some of the longest, most beautiful silver hair I've ever seen framing her teardrop-shaped eyes. Ever since we arrived, she has seemed at home in this place.

"Oh, yeah," I say, snapping out of my thoughts. "Sorry. I'm just thinking everything over."

"If you don't mind me saying, you look a little bit distraught," she continues. Gary, the middle-aged man sitting next to her, nods as if to agree with her.

"I don't know if distraught is the right word," I chuckle. "I'm just thinking of, you know, what's next and everything."

Because right now, right here, I feel oddly at peace. But when I imagine what's next—going back to my lonely apartment and doing, I don't know what, while I try to attain some sense of mental fortitude—that peace shatters.

Is this part of the process? I don't know. All I know is that I long to be in Logan's arms, and I thought it would have been easier by now, but it's not.

And I'm wondering if he's faring any better than me.

Chapter 25

The ringtone pulls me out of my sleep in a dazed surprise; half-blind, I fumble to reach my phone on my nightstand. Who could be calling at such an hour— Oh. It's 11 a.m.

Sophie's name is on the caller ID. Strange. It's not like her to call. She'll usually text me if she wants to chat or even see me. We're millennials, after all.

I answer straight away with a groggy voice: "Hello?"

"Hi! Oh, shit, did I wake you?"

"No? Maybe?"

"Dude, it's 11 a.m."

I sigh and try to rub the sleep from my eyes. "Yeah, I know." Waking up without an alarm has been a part of my 'healing journey', or whatever I want to call it. Since I'm only working with Prakriti Mountain Wellness right now, and their deadlines are pretty loose, I don't have a ton of work to

catch up on. This gives me plenty of time to just … be.

I could have taken on extra contracts, especially with the inquiries coming my way. But right now, I'm choosing simplicity.

To be honest, just 'being' has involved a lot of sleep and lying in bed, questioning my decision to break up with Logan.

"Well, I'd say sorry for waking you, but I don't really feel sorry." I chuckle at that. Of course she wouldn't. Sophie hasn't gotten to truly sleep in three years. "Actually, I'm calling because I need a huge favour."

"Oh?" I perk up. I hardly ever get the chance to help her out, but if she's asking for once, I'm not going to say no.

"How quickly can you be at my house?"

"Um …" I mentally calculate the time it's going to take me to get dressed and look halfway decent, plus drive there. "Forty-five minutes, maybe?"

"Okay. Great."

"Why? What's up?"

"Something came up. Matthew's at work, and I need emergency babysitting for a few hours, STAT. I've got enough pumped milk to keep Heather fed for much longer than I'll be gone."

My heart skips a beat. "Is everything okay?"

"Yes, no worries. I can tell you all about it when you get here. Is that okay?"

I smile. I'm up for this challenge. "Of course, Soph. I'll be right over."

"*Thank you,*" she almost yells in her phone. "You're a lifesaver. Okay, see you soon, then."

I don't waste any time getting ready. I quickly brush my teeth, pull my hair into a messy bun without even brushing through it first, and grab the first outfit I see in my drawer. It's a ratty Avenged Sevenfold T-shirt I've had since high school and some jean shorts. Good enough for babysitting. And I can make myself some coffee once I get to Sophie's place.

Because it's close to noon on a weekday, there's hardly any traffic to drive all the way to Verdun, so I make it there in good time. I park in front of the house and hurry to her door, still secretly hoping everything is okay.

Sophie greets me with a big grin and ushers me in. "Awesome, you're here!" Weird. There's something off about her smile. She almost seems too happy. Why would she—

And that's when I see him and freeze.

Logan is sitting at Sophie's kitchen table, holding Heather in his arms. His eyes are already staring right at me. My chest constricts. Seeing him like this is a shock to my entire system.

What's going on?

A rush of warmth and ice spreads through my limbs all at once. He shouldn't be here. But now that he is, I can't ignore what seeing him is doing to me. Especially the way he's holding Sophie's daughter. It looks so natural on him, and this tableau is beautiful, and *he* is beautiful, and—

I realize I've been standing there, my mouth half open like an idiot. I look back at Sophie, who's smirking, then back at Logan, whose eyes are lit up and warm. "What ..." The words won't come out.

Sophie strides to meet Logan and grabs Heather from his arms. "I can't say I'm too surprised by your reaction," she says with a chuckle. Now that Logan's arms are free, he stands, seeming unsure of where to go. He's motionless by the table, one hand on it as if to steady himself, and I'm still by the door, a good fifteen feet away. "Maybe I should explain."

"But—the babysitting—the—" I stammer, unable to put words together.

"I figured that would be the easiest way to get you here without any argument," Sophie explains as she starts rocking her daughter. "Because here's the thing, Avery. When you told me about everything with Logan right here,"—she gives him a soft tap on the shoulder—"it didn't sit right with me at first, but I didn't know why. And when you left for that retreat, I thought it over. And you know what conclusion I came to?"

"What?" I keep looking from her to Logan. But his gaze is steady. He hasn't taken his eyes off of me, not even for a split second.

"That excuse you gave for breaking it off? It's bullshit." A dagger pierces through my chest. "And you and I both know it."

"What? I don't—" I get out a few more incomplete words.

"So I reached out to Logan to get his opinion. And, well …" she looks at him and backs away. "I'll let you do the honour, Logan." She then proceeds to stride out of the room, leaving Logan and me completely alone.

Logan takes a step forward. I don't move yet. "I'm not going to call what you said bullshit," he starts. Hearing his voice is like warm honey. I close my eyes as if to steady myself. He takes another step forward. "But Sophie's not entirely wrong."

I gather my thoughts. It shouldn't be this hard to speak. I puff up my chest. I need to stay strong. "Logan …" my voice trails off.

Wow. What a great start.

Logan takes yet another step forward. I both want to close the gap between us and run away as far as I can at the same time. "And, okay. Maybe you are sort of fucked up, and maybe I'm not quite right, either. Maybe we both need a bit of healing. I'm not going to argue against that. Don't we all?" Another step. I'm still frozen in place. "And you're right that you might push hard sometimes. You might snap, and you might panic, and you might say or do hurtful things. And you know what? It might be difficult for me to hear. That much is true. All of it is true."

He takes another step, and now he's close enough for me to touch. I can feel the warmth emanating from him. His scent. I take a deep inhale, unable to help myself.

God, all I want is to bury my face in his chest.

But I can't. I'm not done yet. I've still got a lot of shit to figure out. And I don't want to hurt him again.

"But you know what?" Another step. Our bodies are touching now. The contact sends a tingle all the way from my chest to my toes. I have to tilt my head up to look at him. He pulls a loose lock of hair away from my face and tucks it behind my ear, and I shiver.

"I would rather you go through all of that shit with me."

I close my eyes. "Logan …"

Why am I unable to say anything except his name?

He presses a finger against my lips. "If you're going to say you don't want to hurt me, I don't want to hear it. I can take responsibility for my own feelings, Avery. I'm a big boy. So I don't care how messed up you think you are. Hell, I'm a mess, too. And I think we're both smart enough to work through it. Together."

A thousand words want to come out of my mouth at once. He cups the side of my face and continues before I can speak; it's like he can read my mind. "Look, we tried your way. And I can't say for certain that this is how you feel, but I'm going to speak for myself." His thumb brushes my cheek ever so softly, and I shiver again. "It sucked, okay? I fucking hated it. I want to figure my shit out with you by my side. And ..."

For the first time, his gaze falters, and I can see a hint of fear pass through his eyes. "And if you don't feel the same as I do ... if being alone for the past few weeks truly has been working out for you, and you'd rather continue that way ..." His eyes finally meet mine again. They're looking straight into me. "If you can look me in the eye and tell me that, then I'll leave you alone. I'll go my own way and I'll respect your decision. I promise you that." His hand caressing the side of my face is so tender. "But something tells me that this hasn't been the case. And I don't want you to lie just because you think you're protecting me. So tell me the truth, Avery."

For a moment, we only look at each other. Time is standing still. I'm holding my breath as a million thoughts race through my head.

I want to run away. And I know he can see this. He can see I'm scared, that I think I'm going to mess it all up and do something to hurt him again.

It would be the easy way out. All I'd have to do is back away. Tell him no. Tell him I'm too broken for this to work. That the past few weeks have been fine, thank you very much.

But it would be a lie.

And what if he's right? Maybe it's not such a big deal if I haven't taken all the time alone I need. And what if I never feel ready? What if that time never comes? What else am I going to wait for?

Am I going to wait until he gets tired of waiting? Until someone else finally discovers this gem of a man and claims him for herself?

Absolutely not.

I don't speak; instead, I tilt my head up, and our lips meet.

He sighs against my mouth, and I do the same. Instantly, his arms are behind my back, scooping me closer, and I allow myself to do what I've truly been craving ever since we said our goodbyes. I melt into him, weave my hands into his hair, inhale his scent, and gasp against his mouth.

"I love you," he sighs, breaking the kiss long enough to whisper those three small words that I know he means with all his heart.

"I love you, too," I whisper back. "You're right. You're completely right. It sucked. Maybe there's something to be said about learning how to be alone and feeling satisfied as your own person, but right now, I don't care. I missed you too much."

"God, I missed you too, Avery. Let's not do this again."

I laugh, our mouths still touching. "But where are we going to live? And your work? What about—"

"We'll figure it out." He scoops the back of my head and entwines his fingers in my hair underneath my messy bun, threatening to unravel it the way he has unravelled me. "I don't care where we go or what I do. I just want you along with me."

I press my forehead against his and close my eyes. "Me, too."

Epilogue

"Coffee?" Logan's voice brings me back down to Earth. I was so lost in thought that I'm not even seeing my laptop anymore. I blink a few times and look away from my screen to see him standing in front of me.

I can't help but chuckle. He's dressed exactly like a tourist would be, Hawaiian shirt and everything. But he seems so laid back and at ease that I don't even care. Besides, I don't think we're leaving the villa today.

The villa we're staying in at the heart of Ubud, Bali, isn't the most impressive thing in the world. It doesn't have the infinity pool you see in all the cool photos, and it's not facing the ocean like my cabin was in Cape Breton a year ago. But it's cozy, it's clean, and right now, it feels like home. And if that isn't enough, nothing will ever be.

"I'm sorry, I couldn't hear you over the gaudiness of your

shirt," I say, still laughing.

"What?" Logan spreads out his arms to showcase his full outfit. "You don't like it? I think I'm going to keep dressing like this forever."

"Oh my God, don't," I laugh, right before I grab his collar and pull him down for a kiss. I close my eyes and savour this moment. I can't get enough of this. Of him.

I taste the coffee on his tongue and recall what he asked me. "No coffee for me right now," I say as he straightens back up. "When do you start work?"

"In an hour or so." He leaves the airy living room to grab me a coffee from the kitchen.

I take a deep breath. There was once a time when hearing about Logan working would make panic rise out of me. When he announced he was going freelance with his programming work, I instantly thought it was a bad idea. If a regular job had burned him out, the stress of freelancing would tear him apart, I was sure of it.

But I'd been wrong. With a few pointers from me on how to get clients, Logan has been thriving in this lifestyle. Plus, he doesn't have to work nearly as hard to make the same salary he was making before. So whenever he feels himself getting too close to the edge, he just takes on fewer projects.

Which is exactly why I'm not scared anymore. He knows himself, and on days when it feels hard, he's got me. And vice versa.

Anyway, I've got something new to be scared about. But I tell myself it's going to be fine. Of course it will be.

At first, I was scared of falling back into the same spiral

I'd been in the summer before. To be honest, maybe it would happen again. But a year into our time together, it doesn't scare me so much anymore. Plus, the way we constantly move from place to place, taking our work with us, keeps me fully inspired.

Most days aren't full of adventure. On days like today, we spend most of our time on our laptops, catching up on work. Some days, we might get a chance to take a stroll through the jungle, or go for a dip at the beach, or mingle with the locals at a bar or café nearby.

But today, we don't do that. Today, we stay in, and I prepare a dinner of pesto pasta and shrimp, which we eat together as we exchange comments about whatever work pet peeve we want to vent about. Today, I hold something inside of me until it feels like the right moment. But as we're cuddling on the hammock out on the porch, Logan senses that I'm hiding something.

He's holding me against his chest, and he peers down at me, slightly amused. "What is it?" he asks.

"What? Huh?"

"Nuh-huh." He presses me closer. "You're all weird. What are you thinking?"

Today, I sigh and roll my eyes with giddy excitement before I get out of the hammock. I run back to the bathroom where I've hidden what I have yet to show him, and come back quickly before I lose my nerve.

And today, I make Logan cry for the second time when I show him the positive pregnancy test I'm holding in my hand.

Before I realize what's happening, he's holding my face

with both hands, peppering me with kisses everywhere. He's laughing and crying at the same time. An overwhelming bubble of joy bursts in my chest, and now I'm crying, too, kissing him back with all the love that's within me.

"I love you," he sighs against my mouth. One hand touches my belly softly. "Both of you."

"I love you, too."

In this moment, I have everything I've ever wanted. I've never had so much love and laughter in my life before … or maybe I once did, when Logan was a part of my life, all those years back.

And even if it's not perfect—and even though I know this journey will trigger my anxiety in new ways—I wouldn't have it any other way. Because I have Logan by my side. My rock.

And I know he will keep me steady through it all.

Interested in diving into Sophie's love story?

Fall Into You, the next installment of Seasons of the East Coast, will feature Sophie as she finds her own happily ever after through the trials and tribulations of single motherhood.

Sign up for Charlène's newsletter for an exclusive sneak peek into the first chapter of Sophie's adventure, as well as first dibs on beta readings, launch promos, and more!

www.irisbookspublishing.com/pages/newsletter

And if you enjoyed reading this book, please consider leaving an honest review! Reviews are the lifeblood of indie authors, and I'd be incredibly grateful if you took your valuable time to share your opinion.

If you'd like to share a review directly on the book website, you can do so by going to:

www.irisbookspublishing.com/products/summer-kind-of-love

Acknowledgements

As someone who has struggled with anxiety for the better part of her life, writing Avery's journey was part healing and part gut-wrenching.

While Avery is not me, and while her story is not quite mine, we still share some painfully similar traits and experiences that made the writing of this book both cathartic and hell on Earth. Both sweet and bitter. Both painful and relieving.

Those of you who know my journey will know this book is not my first attempt at publishing. (For your sanity, and for my dignity, please don't read my past books. I beg you.) But it is my first time writing something so deeply personal and raw.

I used to write fantasy—not because they were the stories I deeply wanted to tell—but because I think part of me wanted to avoid the vulnerability of telling more realistic stories. And for allowing me to finally uncover the stories that need to be told above any others within me, there is one person alone to thank: my best friend Élissa, who opened the door to a new side of reading I'd never dared to venture into.

Without lending me the book that started my tiptoe into the world of contemporary women's lit, which then took me further into romance, the book you're holding in your hands would not exist. I'm talking about *La fois où … j'ai suivi les flèches jaunes* by Amélie Dubois. (To my anglophone readers, that would be The Time I Followed the Yellow Arrows, which is unfortunately not available in English. Sorry, loves.)

So thank you, my friend, for helping me discover this beautiful world. And thank you for being the first to believe I could write in this genre.

Even though this book is published independently, making it happen was far from an 'independent' venture! I would like to thank Sierra Ward for an absolutely stunning illustration for the cover of this book, Books and Mood for the beautiful exterior and interior design, the amazing duo at Archetype for all the branding and marketing support, and Melissa of Dark Grove Press for polishing up this manuscript with a fine-toothed comb. Last, but certainly not least … Swati, you amazing human. Not only did you whip my manuscript into shape and help me uncover what was missing, but you gave me hope that it could become an amazing book. Now it's in the hands of the readers (yes, you, reading these words right now), and thanks to your relentless cheerleading and coaching, I feel steady and at peace, no matter what happens. You're a wonderful editor AND coach AND marketing advisor AND overall human—which I'm pretty sure makes you some kind of unicorn. A million thanks to you.

I'd also love to thank the very first friend I made on Bookstagram: Kate Cole, who took the first step in connecting with me as a fellow Canadian indie author … this awkward introvert is very thankful to you!

And Mom. I know reading English books isn't your forte. But I must still insert a bit here for you. Your unwavering support no matter what I tackle throughout my life is the reason I have the strength to do what I do. Thank you, thank you, thank you.

Of course, this list wouldn't be complete without mentioning my partner, Jay. You always believed in me, even when writing twenty words a day felt insurmountable. Your love and support are the flame that fuels the romance in not only this book, but every book I write thereafter.

And finally ... thank YOU, reader, for picking up this book—a debut book from an indie author, which I realize is not the easiest sell! I am infinitely grateful that you gave this book a chance, and that you're allowing me to live the dream I've always held close to my heart.

About the Author

Charlène Boutin writes swoon-worthy stories that will make you laugh, cry, and most of all, will warm your heart. Originally from Val-d'Or, Québec (Canada), she spent six years in Red Lake, Ontario, and six more years in Montréal, Québec, giving her fodder for both small-town AND city-driven love stories. She now lives in Granby, Québec, with her partner, son, and tuxedo cat, Clapton. When she's not reading or writing, you'll find her boulder climbing or spending quality time with her family.